JOHN RUSSELL FEARN'S
THE GOLDEN AMAZON

PRIMORDIAL WORLD

JOHN RUSSELL FEARN'S
THE GOLDEN AMAZON

PRIMORDIAL WORLD

JOHN GLASBY

The Golden Amazon, Book 25

WILDSIDE PRESS

INTRODUCTION

Once again it is my privilege to introduce yet another new Golden Amazon adventure by John Glasby, the 25th title in this Wildside reboot series chronicling the interstellar exploits of the Cosmic Crusaders.

Following my own posthumous collaboration with John Russell Fearn, *Chameleon Planet*, #21 in the chronology, famed British writer John Glasby was invited to continue the exploits of Fearn's most famous character. John's new novels comprised *Seetee Sun*, *The Crimson Peril* and *The Sun Movers*, published as numbers 22, 23, and 24 respectively. *Primordial World*, #25, is John's fourth Amazon continuation, and is a full-length 40,000-word novel. Sadly, following his death in 2010, it is also his last, and the last in the series to date. Originally, it was published in a special edition limited to only 100 copies.

In my earlier introductions, I detailed how John Glasby's writing career had striking parallels with that of Fearn. Thus, his Amazon novels exhibited a real "feel" for Fearn's characters, and his plotting closely follow the traditions that Fearn had established. But from his very first Amazon novel, John brought an extra dimension to these new stories, one that was entirely his own. As a fellow of the Royal Astronomical Society and former Director of the British Astronomical Society, he had an encyclopaedic knowledge of astronomy and cosmogony. His science fiction writing was suffused with a real sense of wonder, born of his scientific knowledge and enthusiasm for his subject.

This final novel had an intriguing premise, which allowed the author to exhibit his love of astronomy to the full: The galaxy had formed some five or six billion years ago, but somewhere, there had to be a world where the first intelligent life had evolved.

The Crusaders encounter an alien archeologist, Curtar, whose lifelong work has been to search for that legendary primordial world—Derevan, the first planet in the entire galaxy where the first race had evolved. Curtar has discovered ancient writings suggesting that this race became virtually immortal and possessed all the secrets of the universe. This discovery is known to others of Curtar's race, and there is a faction amongst them who are also seeking the primordial world. They believe they can gain the ancient knowledge that will enable them to gain immortality and the means to subjugate all the races in the galaxy. So the Crusaders join Curtar in the race to discover the primordial world first, to thwart these evil ambitions…

Their quest takes them across thousands of light years, visiting several strange planets, before they find their goal, and a surprising denouement.

John Glasby's colourful adventure novel was another fascinating and worthy final capstone to the saga of the Cosmic Crusaders, which no fan of the Amazon can afford to miss!

—Philip Harbottle,
Wallsend, 2023

CHAPTER I

ABNA, the seven-foot blond giant, husband of the Golden Amazon, stood in front of the energy converter, a worried frown on his handsome features. Some ten minutes earlier, the Ultra had emerged from the four-dimensional continuum and was now traveling at the speed it had entered—a little below half light speed. Since the Ultra's hyperdrive had been modified it was now possible for them to enter hyperspace at any velocity. There was no longer any need to approach light velocity to infuse the vessel with the required energy warp.

The other members of the Cosmic Crusaders were also awake, busily checking the various instruments. Once she was certain that the Ultra was still on the pre-programmed course, the Amazon walked over to where Abna stood. One look at his face and she knew that something was wrong.

Before she could speak, he turned and said gravely, "Something we hadn't bargained for must have happened while we were in hyperspace, Vi. That's why the master computer overrode our pre-set program and awakened us early, ten minutes ago. I inserted our last two copper blocks into the energy converter before we slipped into the four-dimensional continuum. The transition should have only consumed half a block but according to the instruments there's now less than a block left. This has never happened before, and I can find no explanation for it."

"Surely that can't be right." The Amazon bent forward to check the readings although she knew before she looked that Abna would not have made such a mistake. When she straightened up, her expression was as grave as his. She tapped the glass casing with her finger, but the needle remained where it was. "There doesn't seem to be anything wrong with the reading."

"The only thing I can suggest is that, while in hyperspace, we passed very close to a pulsar or a black hole."

Having finished their checks, the others came over. Thania, the latest recruit to the small group, asked, "What exactly does that mean?

Could either of them cause any effects in the fourth continuum? Such a thing has never happened before, has it?"

Abna shrugged his broad shoulders. "It's possible. Both objects produce tremendously powerful gravitational fields, especially a black hole. Normally they *don't* impinge on hyperspace, but there's still a lot we don't know about the four-dimensional continuum. Certainly, we know that material objects are not limited to the velocity of light as in ordinary space. It may be that gravity, which distorts normal space can also produce—under certain exceptional conditions—a similar effect in hyperspace. Evidently, we've been unlucky, and got caught in just such a fluke region. If the computer should have sensed such a powerful gravitational field almost directly ahead, even while in hyperspace, it would take a lot of energy to escape from it."

Thania nodded. She had now completely recovered from the strange sickness she had contracted while they had explored that odd artificial grouping of colored suns. The last of the amazonium—element 125, which had accumulated in her brain—had been completely eliminated from her system.

Grimly, the Amazon explained, "This means that unless we find more copper soon, we'll run out of power and that could be catastrophic. We'd be marooned in space, light years from anywhere."

"But we've never had any trouble finding a copper-bearing planet in normal space before. Surely, we just have to find one and—"

Shaking his head, Abna said tautly, "I'm afraid it isn't going to be as easy as that, Thania. At the moment, we're moving through the Dark Rift in Cygnus and there are very few stars in this vicinity. Take a look at the screen."

They all turned towards the huge screen, which showed the scene outside. Here, there was only blackness with just the odd star visible. The Dark Rift was a vast, almost empty lane moving through the Milky Way, dividing it into two streams as seen from Earth.

Briskly, the ever-active Amazon said, "Well, there's no point standing around, we have to find a suitable planet—and quickly. Viona—check our exact position and then go through the star charts. We may be lucky and find one in time."

Whilst Viona checked rapidly through the charts, her husband Mexone seated himself at the controls of the telescope, turning the large instrument slowly as he scanned the area in which they found themselves.

Five minutes later, Mexone glanced up from the small screen. "Because our pre-set jump through hyperspace was curtailed, we've emerged prematurely. The result is that the nearest sun is about two hundred light years away! Obviously, we don't have sufficient fuel left now to travel that distance, even through hyperspace."

"That seems to be confirmed by the charts of this region." Viona swung round in her chair. "We seem to be in deep trouble."

Tight-lipped, the Amazon strode across the room to stand in front of the viewing screen, her hands on her hips. "This is something we should have foreseen before we entered hyperspace and headed for this area," she said harshly.

"There's nothing to be gained by panic." Abna walked over to stand beside her. "Whatever it was, it must have been something totally unexpected. There's no way you can foresee something like that being right in our path."

"I'm not panicking, Abna." The Amazon swung sharply to face him. "I'm trying to figure out how this could have happened."

"Quite clearly, whether it was what I've just suggested or something else, it happened while we were in hyperspace, causing some unexplained drain on the Ultra's energy. Before we set the coordinates for this part of the Milky Way, we all agreed there's something odd about the Dark Rift. Back on Earth, the old astronomers were unsure whether it's caused by some dense obscuring matter lying along the plane of the galaxy or whether there really is a paucity of stars here. At least, we've now satisfied ourselves that there really are very few stars in this particular region although there certainly seems to be a lot of dust as well."

"Maybe so," the Amazon nodded. "But that doesn't help us in our present situation."

Abna started to make some remark but at that moment, Mexone called suddenly, "There's something out there. It appeared briefly on the mass detector—something quite big."

Swiftly, the Amazon reached over the control panel, her fingers moving dexterously over the keys as she increased the magnification to maximum. Slowly, she shook her head. "There's nothing visible

—at least nothing within a couple of hundred light years. Is it still there, Mexone?"

There was a puzzled frown on the other's face as he muttered, "No, it's gone. But I'm sure I wasn't mistaken."

From the far end of the control panel, Abna said, "Then it can't be a sun unless it's one of those very rare dead stars which have exhausted all of their fuel."

"Are there such things as dead stars?" Thania asked. "I thought they normally ended their lives as supernovae or black holes."

"It all depends on their mass," Mexone explained, still keeping a close watch on the mass detector. "There are stars which are quite small, dim objects. They are nearly all extremely old stars with very little hydrogen left in their interiors. Their nuclear reactions proceed much more slowly than those of larger suns and produce far less energy. They generally end their lives as small red dwarfs which cool slowly until they emit scarcely any visible light at all. If—" Mexone broke off sharply.

"There it is again!"

"Get a fix on it—quickly," the Amazon snapped. "I need its distance and direction. Whatever it is wandering around in all of this empty space, it might be our only chance of getting more copper. In the meantime, I'll reduce our velocity to a minimum. Since we can't see it I don't want to smash into it but on the other hand I don't want to overtake it and lose it."

Tensed with concentration, Mexone manipulated the controls. Finally, he said with a trace of surprise in his voice, "According to these readings, this object is of planetary size, distance fifty million miles and almost dead ahead."

"Planetary size?" Viona echoed wonderingly. "Then it isn't a dead sun or a large meteor as we would have expected."

Mexone shrugged. "I can't give any exact dimensions until we get a little closer, but I would estimate it's about twice the size of your home-world, Amazon."

With the Ultra now merely cruising forward everyone except Mexone crowded in front of the viewing screen, searching intently for any sign of the strange object. They all knew that if, as seemed probable, this planet would emit no light of its own, it would be extremely difficult to pick it out from the surrounding darkness.

They all had a clear view of the region ahead of them. A handful of stars showed against the dark but the two major bands of the Milky Way, literally teeming with stars, lay some three hundred light years away on either side, only just visible at the edges of the screen.

The Amazon was just peripherally aware of Mexone's voice as he tracked the object.

"We seem to be moving almost parallel with it and catching up fast. Thirty-five million miles—thirty million—twenty-five million."

On the wide expanse of the screen there was still nothing visible. Minutes passed with an agonizing slowness as the tension began to mount. Breaking the taut silence, Abna said: "There's something here that's extremely peculiar. I wouldn't have been surprised to find some meteor wandering around in empty space—or even a lone sun—but not a planet."

"Unless it happened to be the outermost world of a large planetary system some time in the past," the Amazon interjected. "If that were the case, the gravitational pull of the parent sun would be quite weak and a passing encounter with another star would be sufficient to throw it off at a tangent, sending it out into the void."

"That's possible, I suppose," Abna conceded.

Viona suddenly emitted an excited yell and jabbed her finger towards the screen.

"There it is. That faint star there has just disappeared."

"She's right!" the Amazon said tautly. She hesitated for a moment as a fresh thought occurred to her. "Switch the viewer to the infrared. There's just a chance it may show something in that region of the electromagnetic spectrum."

"That's hardly likely, Vi," Abna interjected. "With no accompanying sun, the surface temperature of that world must be close to absolute zero. It won't be emitting any infrared radiation. However—" He switched on the infrared viewer.

There was very little change to the picture on the screen. Several of the stars vanished or dimmed appreciably as nothing but their faint infrared emissions were shown. But to their surprise the tiny disc of the distant planet was clearly visible. It showed a little way to the left of the screen and was clearly growing larger with every passing second.

Mystified, Abna muttered, "That is something I don't understand. It must mean that the surface temperature of that world is at least three hundred degrees above absolute zero!" He stared at the Amazon. "It's about as warm as a summer day on Earth."

Smiling, the Amazon said, "Then apart from the possibility of finding copper there I think this is a mystery worthy of the attention of the Cosmic Crusaders."

Twenty minutes later they were close enough to the strange dark world to make out a few details. The Amazon had delicately operated the controls so that their speed now exactly matched that of the planet. Water was definitely present on the surface but not in the form of oceans even though the planet was almost twice Earth-size. Rather there were a number of large lakes and several rivers.

"Spectrum analysis definitely confirms that that is water," Abna said, pointing. "Also there is an atmosphere and its composition very closely resembles our own so there should be no problems about our breathing it. What puzzles me, however, is how the temperature there can remain so high considering that it's drifting free in empty space with no direct sunlight to warm it."

"The only answer I can think of at the moment is thermal heating from the interior," Viona suggested.

"Is it possible there could be any kind of intelligent life down there?" Thania asked.

"Anything is possible," Abna said. "I don't suppose you've ever heard of orthogenesis?"

The teenager shook her head in obvious bewilderment.

"It's a theory of the mechanism of evolution put forward a few centuries ago. It postulates that evolutionary variation is determined by the action of the external environment on the organism concerned. Put briefly, that means that the possibilities of variation are strictly limited to certain definite lines."

"What Abna means, Thania," the Amazon put in, "is that the form taken by any possible inhabitants of this planet was determined millennia ago when it formed as part of a planetary system very similar to those we know. Any life which may exist down there did not come into existence on this planet when it was in free space."

"Then if there is any life down there, how could they adapt to being plunged so quickly into the depths of interstellar space?"

Mexone queried. Now that the strange world had been picked up by the infrared detector, he got up and joined the others at the screen.

"Firstly," the Amazon explained, "we don't know for certain if there is any life. This could be a completely sterile planet although the present conditions could support life, as we know it. I think the first thing to do now is scan the entire surface from a fairly low altitude. Even if it is devoid of life, we still have to land and find more copper."

"Does that mean we'll get a chance to have a good look around?" asked Viona, ever anxious to be doing something positive. The last few weeks had been boring for her and now she was desperate for some action.

"First things first," the Amazon said admonishingly. "Now let's see what we have here."

Edging the Ultra closer to the planet, Abna put the huge spaceship into an orbit around it. In the weird infrared light, the surface had a strange glow, but details were picked out sharply. There seemed to be few clouds and the atmosphere was completely transparent. The powerful telescope, readily adapted to the different wavelengths, showed the tiniest details.

Everywhere they looked, the surface appeared to be composed of some kind of rock, interspersed by the rivers and lakes. Nowhere did they glimpse any sign of buildings or any indication that life had ever been present.

Finally, the Amazon sank down into her chair, her chin in her hands. "Somehow, I doubt if we'll find anything of interest here. We'll just land and make a search for copper and then be on our way again."

"Aren't you the least bit interested in finding out how the atmosphere can hold this high temperature for so long?" Abna asked. "My guess is that this world has been wandering through empty space for millions of years. In that time some kind of thermal equilibrium would have been reached and the temperature should be much lower. There has to be some kind of continuous heat transfer from the interior."

"It's an interesting point," The Amazon replied. "But our intentions are to help backward and downtrodden races in the galaxy with our scientific knowledge. Clearly there are none here who need our aid. It would simply be a waste of time and energy just studying the kinetics of a dead world."

"Then we're just going to look for copper and then leave?" Víona said in a disappointed tone.

"Unless there is any—" the Amazon began; then stopped abruptly and jerked herself out of her chair, leaning forward. "What's that?" She indicated a small region of the surface close to a range of mountains.

They all stared. Incredibly, there were lights down there on the surface—a small ring of white dots.

"So, this world isn't quite as dead as we thought," Abna muttered softly. He switched the viewing screen back to visible light and deftly tuned a knob, magnifying the small region. Now the crude building was clearly visible and not far away was the unmistakable shape of what was undeniably a spaceship, although one of an unusual design unlike anything they had seen before.

"Any suggestions?" the Amazon asked. "Do we land and introduce ourselves to whoever is down there?"

Viona brushed a strand of her copper-colored hair from her forehead. "I think we should. From the size of that building I'd say there aren't many of them there and we can take care of ourselves if they don't like intruders interrupting whatever they're doing. I'd say that whatever it is it must be important to them, staying on an otherwise empty world."

The Amazon reached a quick decision. "Then we go down—but we'll all go armed." She motioned towards the rack containing their utility belts all equipped with protonic blasters and a variety of other weapons and instruments.

Spearing through the atmosphere with Abna now managing the controls, the Ultra dipped down towards the planet. Being such a skilled pilot, landing the huge spaceship in complete darkness presented no problem. Deftly, he landed the craft within half a mile of the small ring of lights.

A final check had determined that the atmosphere was quite breathable and with the outside temperature so mysteriously high, they did not need their suits. The Amazon was first down the ladder, dropping gently to the ground. Here, the gravity was slightly higher than Earth-type but their superhuman strength made light work of walking.

Cautiously, they made their way over the rough, uneven ground towards the lights. To one side of them was the large hut and in the near distance stood the alien spacecraft—a squat ugly shape with the snouts of projectile launchers jutting from the hull. Even in the darkness it looked rusty and incredibly ancient.

"Some mining pioneer, you think?" Abna said in a low voice. He advanced towards the front of the building. The door stood open and there was only darkness inside. "Well, whoever he is, he's obviously not at home. I wonder where he can be?"

"What makes you think he's alone?" the Amazon commented. "There could be several of them around, probably watching us this very moment, not sure why we're here. I would have thought our approach would have been heard for miles."

"Just a hunch I have," Abna replied. "From what I can see yonder, we've stumbled upon some lone pioneer working this planet for minerals." He pointed to their right.

Now they all made out the dark shadow in the ground some fifty yards away. They approached it cautiously, suddenly finding themselves standing on the lip of a deep shaft.

It was roughly square and at least six feet along each edge. Now they were looking straight down, they noticed the faint light at the bottom and what looked like a makeshift rope or and pulley affair at one side.

Several thick cables ran down the other side and, taking out her torch, the Amazon noticed that these ran along the ground, back to the spaceship. Obviously, these supplied electrical power to some type of machinery deep below the ground.

"What under the stars is this place?" Thania murmured.

"I'm almost certain it's some kind of mining operation," Abna told her. "But to me that light is at least five hundred feet down. It must have taken a prodigious amount of work to sink this shaft. Even with the equipment we have on board the Ultra it would take us a few days to do something like this. But with the antiquated equipment I see here, it must have taken years."

The next moment, a sound reached them from somewhere far below. The light was suddenly extinguished. Beside the Crusaders, the pulley began to turn slowly. Something was coming up from those remote depths.

Stepping back, they moved some distance from the lip of the shaft and drew their weapons, ready to use them at a moment's notice. Ten minutes passed and then the sound of the pulley stopped. The dark shape of a man appeared, stepping over the rim of the shaft and moving towards the building.

The man was halfway to the door when some strange instinct seemed to warn him of their presence. He whirled and his right hand went towards something at his waist. The Amazon did not wait a second longer. At the moment, she wanted him alive. Launching herself forward, she covered the distance between them before the man could draw his weapon.

A hand like steel clamped on his wrist. Uttering a harsh cry, the other dropped the gun. But he was not finished. His left fist struck the Amazon a savage blow on the chin. An ordinary person would have gone down under such an impact—but, as the man soon discovered, the Amazon was not an ordinary woman.

Before he could move, she caught him around the waist, lifted him, and threw him to the ground. Wrenching out her own gun, she covered him as the other Crusaders came running up. Taking out his torch, Abna played the beam over the figure now lying moaning on the ground.

Uttering a faint exclamation of surprise, Viona said, "Why he's a very old man."

In appearance, the man was very similar to a human being, apart from the odd shape of his ears and nose.

"He's still strong enough to pack quite a hefty punch," the Amazon declared. "I think we should get him inside the building and then try to question him." She picked up the weapon and examined it closely in the torchlight. "This looks like some kind of highly sophisticated atomic pistol."

Bending, Abna gripped his fingers tightly in the coat the man wore and pulled him effortlessly to his feet. Getting his hands under him, he carried him through the open door. Going in behind him, the Amazon ran her fingers along the wall and soon located a small switch that she snapped down. Instantly light flooded the interior from two long tubes near the ceiling, extending the whole length of the building.

There was a long table in the middle with a couple of recognizable chairs beside it. A shelf along one wall was piled high with scrolls and there were others arranged neatly on the table. Going to the far end, Viona examined a number of large cases. Turning, she said, "He has a large supply of food pills here and what looks like water-synthesizing equipment. I'd say it's obvious he's been here for some considerable time and probably means to stay quite a lot longer."

Abna had placed the man in one of the chairs. He still seemed to be unconscious, lying half across the table, his head to one side. His untidy white hair and short beard confirmed their first appraisal of him. Quite possibly he was in the region of a hundred years old.

Glancing at Abna, the Amazon said, "If he is some kind of prospector, he may be able to tell us if there's any copper ore here." Biting her lower lip, she paused for a moment; then went on, "I wonder what he's looking for?"

"It must be something pretty important—and valuable," Thania interrupted, "otherwise he wouldn't be living this lonely life, light years from any kind of civilization. And it can't have been easy for him erecting all of this and then digging that huge shaft out there."

The man stirred and lifted his head, a low groan coming from his lips. He grimaced as he put a hand up to his scalp. Then he swung his head quickly, glaring at each of them in turn. For a moment he seemed on the point of getting to his feet. Then his gaze fell on the weapons they carried and he slumped back again. A string of harsh gutturals came from his lips.

"One thing is certain," Mexone observed. "Whatever he's doing here, he isn't very pleased to see us. Probably thinks we're here to steal his find."

The Amazon looked questioningly at her husband. "We won't get very far unless we understand his language or he learns ours. Do you think you can absorb his?" She knew that when under stress Abna could assimilate an entire language in only a few minutes.

Abna ran a hand down his cheek. "Perhaps it would save time if I learned his. We could then take him on board the Ultra and use the Educator so that he can understand English—or I can try to pass his language straight on to all of you."

"Then do that," The Amazon said tightly. "I'm not sure why but there's something here which doesn't quite add up in my mind. I don't know what it is but the sooner we find out, the better."

Drawing his brows down into a straight line, Abna concentrated intently on the man's mind while the others kept their weapons trained on him. Finally, he looked up and gave a slight smile. "It's done," he said softly.

Turning back to the old man Abna spoke rapidly in the other's language. An expression of astonishment crossed the wrinkled features. Then he said something in a torrent of words, still glancing fearfully at the Crusaders.

"What did he say?" the Amazon demanded.

"He wants to know if we come from Kezbek. I presume that's a planet somewhere in this region."

Looking down, Abna conversed with the man, speaking at some length. Watching the man's face closely all the time as the Amazon looked on impatiently. When he had finished, Abna said gravely, "He doesn't want to talk much about what's going on here. He seems to be unduly frightened, and I don't think he believed me when I told him we've never heard of Kezbek, that we come from Earth more than a thousand light years away."

The Amazon pressed her full lips into a hard line. "Quite clearly he's hiding something, and I want to know what it is." While it annoyed her to think that this was one scientific achievement in which Abna was superior to her, she said evenly, "I have to talk to him. Transfer this language to all of us, Abna. The fact that he was armed when he came out of that shaft could mean he's expecting visitors and if that's the case, I want to be forewarned."

"Surely you don't suspect that he's running away from someone, mother?" Viona put in. "It's more likely these 'visitors' are after what he's looking for."

"Whatever the reason, I want to know about it," the Amazon retorted harshly. "Now fill us in on this language, Abna."

"Very well," Abna shrugged. "If you're all ready for it." Concentrating fiercely, he attuned all of their minds to the alien tongue. At length, they had it fully implanted in their minds.

Walking round the table, the Amazon seated herself in the chair opposite the old man, leaning forward and resting her elbows on the rough wood. Her beautiful features were drawn into a determined expression as she said thinly, "I'm going to ask you some questions, old man, and I want truthful answers. Do you understand?"

By now, the other appeared to have accepted that the people who faced him possessed an intelligence superior to his own and his face evinced no surprise as she spoke in his own language. He gave an almost imperceptible nod.

"Good," the Amazon nodded back. "We've already told you that we do not come from Kezbek, wherever that may be. We are from the planet of a sun so far distant you would need a powerful telescope to see it. We mean you no harm, our only intention in landing here is to search for copper which we need as fuel for our spacecraft."

"Copper?"

"That's right. My guess is that you're some kind of prospector, mining this strange planet for some mineral that is highly valuable, gold or uranium perhaps. That would explain why you thought we were enemies coming to steal whatever you've found."

Surprisingly, the man shook his head. "You think I'm a prospector searching for minerals on this world?"

"Well, aren't you?" Mexone asked from the end of the table. "That looks like mining equipment out there and why else would you dig a shaft like that?"

"You're wrong. I'm looking for something far more important than any minerals."

CHAPTER II

THE Amazon experienced surprise at the old man's reply but she quickly recovered herself as her scientific mind took over her emotions. There was indeed a mystery here.

What else, she mused, could exist on this world other than various ores?

From further along the table, Viona asked the question in the Amazon's thoughts. "If you're not digging for minerals or precious stones, what is it you're looking for?"

The old man turned and looked searchingly at her and then at the other Crusaders. Finally, addressing the Amazon, he said, "You say you only landed here to look for copper for your spacecraft. You have nothing to do with those from Kezbek?"

"Nothing at all," the Amazon assured him. "As we told you, we have no knowledge of such a world. Our mission is to travel the galaxy helping any race which is being oppressed—or those we can make their lives better using our scientific knowledge."

The man considered that for more than a minute, scrutinizing them all closely. Finally, he seemed to have reached a decision. "My name is Curtar. Kezbek is my home planet, a world I left more than fifty cycles ago. Like you I am a scientist, but specializing in archaeology. My search is for the primordial world, Derevan, the first planet in the entire galaxy on which life, intelligent life, came into existence."

The Amazon stared at him, momentarily stunned by this revelation. This was something she had never considered before—yet it made sense. The galaxy had formed some five or six billion years ago. Somewhere, there had to be a world where the first race had evolved—but considering the tremendous length of time that had elapsed, it seemed scarcely credible that this race was still in existence.

"You believe that this is that world?" Abna asked. "Is that the evidence you're looking for?"

Curtar shook his head slowly. "Nay, this is not Derevan. That world is still lost—yet before I die, I hope to find it. I've devoted more than eighty cycles searching, reading through ancient archives, following one blind trail after another but never giving up hope."

"Then why are you looking here?"

Curtar sank back wearily into his chair, his eyes clouded. Pointing towards the end of the room, he said hoarsely, "Bring me that red box. I fear it is too long since I have eaten."

Thania crossed the room and brought the box to him. Opening it, he took out a red tablet, placed it on his tongue and swallowed it. After a little while, some of the strength came back into his body. His voice was stronger as he continued, "Long ago, during my researches among the archives on Kezbek, I stumbled upon an extremely ancient parchment. It was inscribed in the old tongue of my people and proved extremely difficult to translate—but finally, I succeeded.

"It contained vague references to Derevan, certainly not sufficient to enable me to locate that world. There was, however, a reference to this race where it was said that they attained the highest possible level of cultural and scientific achievement. They knew all there was to know about the galaxy. There was some writing there to indicate that they may still exist—that they became immortal."

"Immortal?" Viona said. "You mean they live for ever?"

"Yes. So it would seem."

"Yet one thing puzzles me," Mexone interjected. "You're clearly afraid of these others from your home-world. Why is that?"

Curtar swung to look at him and there was a spark in his eyes that had not been there before and an abrupt hardening of his aged features. "Because they learned of my work and they also seek Derevan—but not like me for purely scientific reasons. They wish to find it for power, the power to rule the entire galaxy."

"Power?"

Curtar said solemnly, "According to the ancient writings, this race became virtually immortal and possessed all of the secrets of the universe. They could have conquered the whole of the galaxy had they wished—but this they chose not to do. That is what those among my people are seeking—their incredible knowledge so they can subjugate all races to their will and also become immortal themselves.

"Some half a million cycles into their scientific evolution, however, part of the Derevan race left their planet and traveled here. I don't know the reason for that but if this is true, there should be some of their artifacts, some evidence, still surviving, possibly more of their writings which may allow me to trace back the path they took, all the way back to Derevan."

The Amazon turned this information over in her mind before saying, "One thing still puzzles me. If, as you say, they are virtually immortal, why are they not here now?"

"That is an enigma I've so far been unable to resolve. I can only suggest that something truly drastic happened, hundreds of millions of years ago, something which wiped them out completely."

"A nuclear war?" Viona suggested.

"No, I don't believe that's the answer. When I first came here, I made a thorough check of the planet for radioactivity. Apart from trace amounts, almost certainly due to radioactive ores in the ground, there is nothing."

By now the Amazon's scientific curiosity had been aroused and, glancing at her companions, she knew they felt the same. What she was going to propose, however, was something she was unsure whether Curtar would accept. He had made it absolutely clear that he was afraid of others discovering this knowledge he was searching for and using it for their own avaricious ends.

Speaking calmly and reassuringly, she said, "As scientists, Curtar, we also seek for knowledge. You are old now and have worked here, alone, and still not found what you're looking for. Also, from what we've seen of your spacecraft, I doubt if it would take you through the galaxy, exploring countless star systems, hoping to find one world among billions. With the Ultra, our spacecraft, we can travel far faster than light through hyperspace and cover great distances in a short time."

She instantly noticed the expression of suspicion in his eyes and went on hurriedly, "We do not search for power and dominion over other races. Mere scientific curiosity is the only reason I suggest for helping you."

"Why should I trust you any more than the others?" Suspicion was evident in the old man's voice.

"Because we could have killed you the moment you drew that weapon on us," Mexone said sharply. "We could still do that now we know your language and what your purpose is here."

The Amazon shot him a warning glance, forcing him into silence and then swung her gaze back to Curtar. "Believe me you cannot do this on your own. Furthermore, with our armament we can protect you from these others you speak of."

Curtar thought long and hard about her proposition. It was clear that he was still suspicious but finally he nodded. "Very well. I suppose I must trust someone but—" He broke off in mid-sentence.

A distant scream echoed through the air outside. Rapidly, it grew louder, rising in pitch until it shrieked in their ears.

Curtar thrust himself from his chair, his lined face a mask of fear. "It's a missile!" He screamed the warning. "They must have found me." Before any of the Crusaders could stop him, he was rushing towards the door.

Acting swiftly, the Amazon ushered the others outside and then flicked off the light. The next second there was a vivid flash, and a thunderous explosion rocked the ground beneath their feet. A blast of superheated air swirled around them. Curtar was instantly thrown off his feet and sent tumbling across the hard ground. His limp body struck a boulder and he lay still.

"We have to get back to the Ultra!" Abna shouted loudly. "Here on the ground we're sitting targets. Bring the old man."

The Amazon had already caught her fingers in Curtar's coat. Gripping it tightly, she hauled him upright and then threw him over one shoulder, running swiftly after the others to where the Ultra stood waiting. A second detonation hammered at their ears as they climbed quickly inside. While Mexone slammed the airlock shut, the Amazon carried the old man along the corridor to the control room. Here she deposited his limp body in one of the padded chairs before joining Abna at the controls.

Moments later, the engines started, and the Ultra began to lift, rising swiftly into the air as Abna manipulated the controls.

Without needing to be told, the other Crusaders were at the windows scanning the blackness for any sign of the attackers. Swiftly, the Ultra cleaved through the atmosphere and a few moments later they were in space with the dark, lonely planet hanging in the void beneath them.

"Anyone see anything?" the Amazon called as she scanned the large visiscreen, her keen eyes searching for any sign of the marauding vessels.

"Nothing yet," Thania called back. "If they have no lights showing it won't be easy to spot them unless we can pick out their exhausts. At the moment we don't know how many there are."

Smoothly, Abna turned the nose of the Ultra into an orbit around the world. The darkness around them seemed absolute. Then, suddenly, something caught the Amazon's keen gaze. It was only a small pinprick of light almost directly ahead of them, so small that she almost missed it altogether.

"There's one vessel," she said sharply. Even as she spoke, the speck of light grew brighter and larger.

Abna had spotted it too. Slowly, he increased the velocity. Very soon, it was just possible to make out the shape of the enemy vessel. It looked similar to that which they had seen on the planet but much larger and clearly much better armed. A meticulous survey of the region confirmed that there were no other craft in the area.

"It would seem that our friend here was telling the truth," Mexone observed, "when he claimed there were others after him. My guess is that that ship has come from Kezbek like himself."

Viona broke in excitedly: "It looks as though they've spotted us. They're changing course."

One glance at the screen was enough to tell them this was true. The enemy vessel was veering rapidly to the right in a tight curve.

"Are the repeller screens up?" the Amazon called sharply.

"Up and at full power," Thania answered as she took her place at the armaments controls.

"Good. Then be ready for an attack." Scarcely had the Amazon spoken than a brilliant flash showed halfway along the hull of the other spacecraft.

"Here it comes!" Thania yelled. Without pausing to think she thumbed a couple of buttons in front of her. There was an almost imperceptible lurch as two super-x-hydrogen missiles sped on their unerring way towards the distant spaceship.

The next moment, without any warning, they were all thrown forward with such incredible violence it was impossible to prepare for it. All of the lights went out but none of them had any time in which to work out what had happened before the impacts against the controls and the inner hull thrust them swiftly into unconsciousness. Some tremendous retarding force had gripped the ship in an unbreakable hold, stopping it dead in space. The first impression of which the Amazon was aware was the darkness and complete silence. There was no whine from the mighty engines, no whisper of air from the conditioning units—nothing. Very slowly, she opened her eyes wider. She could see nothing but gradually her eyes adjusted to the utter blackness. All of her senses seemed awry. Since there was absolute silence, she guessed that the others had suffered the same fate as she had and were all still unconscious.

None of them were moving, nor was the Ultra. To her bemused senses, they seemed to be hanging motionless in space. Savagely, she forced herself to recall what had happened. Something from that enemy vessel had hit them—and the next moment, everything had stopped. After that, she could remember nothing—it was all a complete blank.

For a few moments she lay still, struggling to collect her bemused thoughts. None of the automatic alarms were sounding which indicated that there had been no major damage. Clearly, whatever had hit them had not been explosive or atomic in nature. So what could it have been?

Placing her hands flat on the floor, she somehow pushed herself up onto her arms. In spite of the pain in her hands and back, she managed to get onto her hands and knees. There still seemed to be Earth-gravity in operation but the air was oddly stale, biting at the back of her throat, and getting gradually worse. Very slowly, she inched her way to the controls.

Relying solely on touch, she managed to locate the small compartment that contained the spare torches, knowing that until she had light of some kind there was little she could do.

Switching on the torch, she flashed the powerful beam around the control room. As she had surmised, all the others were still unconscious. Abna was slumped forward over the controls, one hand out and his head resting against two of the levers. Feeling the pulse in his neck, she found it was still beating strongly. Moving his arm slightly, she flicked down the switch to start the engines. Nothing happened! They seemed to be completely dead. No power at all was reaching them! Desperately she tried again but with the same result.

On the viewing screen there was now no sign of the enemy ship. The strange planet was still visible far below them, turning slowly on its axis.

A sudden movement bought her swinging round. Near the hull, Thania was stirring and a few moments later, Viona rolled over onto her side blinking against the brilliant torchlight. Her eyes were wide as she stared up at her mother.

It was Viona who spoke first, getting one arm under her. "What happened? It felt as though we had ran into a brick wall."

Helping Viona to her feet, the Amazon crossed to Thania. Surprisingly, the teenager appeared unharmed apart from a couple of bruises and it was evident the padded chair had saved her from more serious injury.

"I don't know what happened," the Amazon replied with a puzzled frown. "We seem to be stuck in space. Nothing works—the engines can't be started, and all of the lights are off."

"And there's something wrong with the air," Thania said, coughing hoarsely.

A few moments later, Mexone lifted his head. Almost instantly a spasm of pain crossed his features as he moved his right leg.

"Lie still." The Amazon went down on one knee beside him, handing the torch to Thania. Gently, she ran her hands over his leg. "It seems to be broken, I'm afraid," she told him at last "Abna is still unconscious. He must have hit his head on the control panel. Once he comes round, when he feels up to it, he'll take a look at you."

"How is our hermit friend?" Viona asked as the Amazon straightened up.

"By the stars, I'd forgotten all about him." Swiftly, she eased her way across the floor with Thania beside her. Curtar had apparently been flung out of his chair by the sudden halt and now lay sprawled on the floor beside it. Bending, she felt his neck for the pulse. Thankfully, it was still beating and she guessed that, being unconscious at the time, his body had simply slid limply to the floor like an empty sack.

Lifting him easily, she placed him back in the chair and then turned her attention to Abna. He was still breathing normally but it was several minutes before he regained consciousness, thrusting himself straight in the seat. He ran a hand across his forehead, a dazed look in his eyes.

"Did we hit something?" he asked slowly, "Or did something hit us—a bomb, perhaps? I've never known anything like that happen before." He looked round. "How are the others?"

"They don't appear to be badly hurt except for Mexone. I suspect his right leg is broken."

Sucking in a deep breath, Abna nodded. "Don't worry about that. Once I've pulled myself together, I'll fix that."

The Amazon went to a cupboard and brought out a small box. It contained a hypodermic and several glass phials each containing a powerful restorative solution. Swiftly, she injected them all in turn.

Ten minutes later, employing his fantastic metaphysical powers, Abna had Mexone's leg as good as new. By now, Curtar had also regained his senses and was sitting bolt upright at the table, still trying to piece together how he had got there.

At the control panel, Abna stood with his face twisted into a mask of incomprehension. He shook his head slowly. "I still don't understand it. Something must have stopped the engines but if that had been the case, we should still be moving. Our momentum would continue to carry us forward. Instead, we're just hanging here in space."

"Not only that," the Amazon interjected, "but nothing appears to be operating. Even the air conditioning has failed. If we don't sort this out soon, the air in here will be unbreathable."

She did not notice that Curtar had risen from his chair and joined them until he spoke. "I think I can explain what has happened. Tell me, did you find that Kezbek vessel which launched those missiles?"

Abna nodded. "We spotted its exhaust and were closing in when it opened fire on us."

"What exactly did you see?"

"It was just a brilliant flash from somewhere halfway along the hull," Thania remarked.

"Then that is the explanation. They used a stasis bomb against you, possibly more than one. Such a weapon forms a—how shall I say it?—bubble of space around you wherein everything is static. Inside that, your spaceship is held motionless and none of your instruments will operate."

"You've come across such a weapon before?"

Curtar nodded in affirmation. "They use it whenever they encounter an enemy whose weapons, they believe are far superior to theirs. It gives them a chance to escape. From what you say, they fled. Perhaps they are still somewhere on the planet for they will never give up until they have captured me and forced me to tell then everything of my work."

"Does that mean we're doomed to hang here forever—or at least until our air gives out?" Thania cried, a note of anxious alarm in her voice.

"How long such a field will remain in existence depends upon a number of factors," Curtar explained. "It requires a lot of energy to create this stasis field and maintain it in existence. These fields are extremely unstable. Did any of you see what happened to the Kezbek ship? If it is still close by they can undoubtedly continue to inject energy into this weapon. If not, then there may be a chance it will decay in a relatively short time."

They all shook their heads. Viona said, "One minute we were watching it on the screen and the next we all blacked out."

"But I did manage to fire two super-x-hydrogen missiles," Thania interrupted excitedly. "I'm quite sure they were both on target."

Abna struck the control panel with his fist. "Of course, you did, Thania! Then unless their weapon interfered with them, which is unlikely because of their propulsion system, my guess is that the Kezbek vessel has been destroyed—or at least badly damaged."

"That being the case," Curtar said reassuringly, "I would say this stasis field will almost certainly decay within an hour or so."

Time now passed agonizingly slowly for those on board the Ultra. Every five minutes, Abna tried to start the engines but each time with no success. All the time the air inside the cabin was become more and more stale. Around them, the eerie silence grated on nerves drawn as taut as steel wires.

In the darkness, with only the torch to provide any light, it was difficult to do anything. All they could do was crowd around the controls as Abna struggled to get them moving again. Outside, there was nothing to see. The stasis bubble that held them completely immovable was totally invisible. All of them were used to the faint whine of the engines to provide a background noise but with that no longer present the clinging silence became more and more oppressive.

Then, at the tenth attempt, the engines stuttered as Abna pressed the button. For a moment, it seemed they were on the point of roaring into life—but a few seconds later, they failed again.

Standing near the back of the small group, Curtar said tightly, "The force field must be weakening. Take it from me it will not be long now before everything is back to normal."

"I only wish I had your confidence," Viona muttered as a spasm of coughing seized her. "We seem to have been hanging here for an eternity."

Without turning his head, Abna said crisply, "Once the engines do start, two of you had better man the armaments. If that Kezbek vessel wasn't destroyed, they may be lying in wait for us. I don't want to be taken by surprise a second time."

Immediately, Mexone and Thania made their way across to the weapon controls. Dim shadows in the torchlight, they sat tensed in their seats, hands ready on the keys.

Drawing in a deep breath, Abna said, "Well, here goes." He thumbed the button. The next second, several things happened at once. The engines burst into uproarious life sending a slight shudder through the ship, the lights came on again and very slowly, the air began to freshen.

Smiling broadly, the Amazon said, "We seem to be operational again. It would appear you were right, Curtar, about that weapon. Now to see what's happened down on the surface."

CHAPTER III

THEY landed smoothly on the small plateau close to Curtar's drilling site half an hour later. Descending onto the rocky surface, they used more powerful portable searchlights to determine what damage had been caused by the enemy bombardment. Soon, it became obvious that the Kezbekians had not intended to damage or destroy either the building or the immensely deep shaft. Apparently, they had merely wanted to flush Curtar out into the open and then capture him.

Two huge craters had been blasted out of the ground by atomic missiles but both of these were more than two miles from the site.

"Evidently those people wanted you alive," the Amazon remarked. "It's also clear they wanted to know what you've discovered down there. Those nuclear bombs were just a warning to you not to put up a fight once they landed."

"So it would seem," Curtar nodded. "And without your timely help they would have confiscated everything and taken me back to Kezbek."

"Where you would undoubtedly have been tortured and made to reveal everything," Abna added grimly.

"That is true," Curtar admitted. "They will go to any lengths to get their hands on my notes and examine what I've found down there. Even though my information is sadly incomplete, it would not take them too long to decipher the inscriptions at the bottom of the shaft. They would merely have to visually record them and study them at their leisure."

Before the old man could go on, the Amazon said, "I think we can talk better inside. There's no chance of anyone taking us by surprise. I've set the automatic scanning device on the Ultra. It will give me warning on this,"—she took a small instrument from her belt—"if any spaceship approaches within two thousand miles."

Inside the building, Curtar seated himself wearily in his chair and motioned the Amazon to the one opposite. There being no other seats, the rest of the Cosmic Crusaders stood around the walls except for Viona and Thania, who sat on the edge of the bed against the wall.

"What is it you want to know?" the old man asked. "I will tell you everything I can."

"Firstly," said the Amazon, "something which has puzzled us since we first came upon this world. It has no parent sun and must have been traveling alone through empty space for many years, yet the temperature outside is about 26 degrees. How is that possible?"

Curtar gave a wry smile. "It's really very simple. From what I can discover, this world has been without a sun for more than three hundred million years since the Derevanians came here. Being of planetary mass, it has probably always had an atmosphere. It also possesses a molten core and they used that to heat the atmosphere through large ducts in the surface."

"I guess that answers that question," Viona remarked, swinging her legs slightly.

"Secondly," the Amazon went on, "do you know where there may be copper ores so that we might replenish our fuel supply?"

Curtar nodded. "I made a few preliminary drillings before I hit upon this one. There is copper ore here often in quite large quantities. As for what I've found down there, I suggest that waits until we have eaten something and then rested. Since there is neither night nor day on this planet, I eat when I'm hungry and sleep when I'm tired."

"An excellent philosophy," Abna commented.

"However there is something I would like to show you first. I think you'll all find it extremely interesting."

Getting up from his chair, Curtar made his way to a small door set in the far wall. Going inside, he motioned to the others to follow him. He flicked a small switch and light came on from a small bulb set near the low ceiling.

By comparison with the main room, this one was quite small. There was a desk in the middle and a couple of shelves around two of the walls. Going over to one of them, he took down something and brought it over to them, handing it to the Amazon.

It was a small statuette made from a strange green stone that was peculiarly heavy. Peering over the Amazon's shoulder, Abna remarked, "An ugly-looking devil. What is this supposed to represent?"

The figurine was of a creature sculptured in a crouching pose. Two large wings sprouted from between its shoulders and the features had a strange, almost bird-like look with a pointed beak. The eyes, however, were situated at the front of the face and not as the sides as with normal birds.

"My guess is that this is an image of a Derevanian," Curtar said quietly. "I suppose he does look ugly by our standards."

"I would say that unlike any bird species I'm aware of, those eyes have stereoscopic vision like humans," the Amazon remarked.

"So you believe the Derevanians were an avian species?" Víona put in.

"Why not?" the Amazon answered. "On Earth, the dinosaurs ruled the planet for over two hundred million years and then became extinct towards the end of the Cambrian Period some 65 million years ago—except for the flying species which later developed into birds. It was then, however, that the mammals took over finally evolving into mankind. I see no logical scientific reason why on Derevan, it was a flying species which became dominant."

Replacing the statuette, Curtar said, "I suggest we rest now. Tomorrow you can see at first hand what the Derevanians left behind."

* * * *

Twelve hours later—Earth-time—they had already made plans. While Abna, Mexone and Thania returned to the Ultra having been directed by Curtar where to locate the nearest drilling which would provide them with a plentiful supply of copper ore, the Amazon and Viona were to accompany Curtar down the shaft.

Once the Ultra had blasted off, Curtar led the duo to the edge of the gaping hole. All three carried powerful torches. By their light, the Amazon noticed the large, latticed cage at one side attached to the pulley. It looked fragile in the torchlight.

"Are you sure this can take our combined weight?" Viona queried dubiously.

"There's no need to be afraid," Curtar assured them. "It's quite safe." He waited until the two had stepped through the gate in one side; then lowered himself into it. Viona held onto the side with a white-knuckled grip as it swayed precariously.

Then Curtar thrust a small lever into place, and they were descending slowly into the black depths. As they went down, their guide shone the beam of his torch on the rock walls enclosing them.

"Being scientists, I'm sure you both know something of archaeology." His voice sounded oddly hushed, echoing eerily from the rock sides of the shaft. "You can readily make out the different strata we're passing through until we reach the bottom. By then we will be more than three billion in the past. It isn't difficult to date each stratum and as you see, there is no indication of life at present. We must go down much further than this to find that."

"And you did all of this by yourself?" The Amazon could not conceal her surprise.

Curtar nodded. "It took me some twenty cycles to locate this world and a further thirty to excavate all of this."

In spite of her usual lack of emotion, the Amazon could not help feeling a deep admiration for this man and his total dedication to his self-appointed task. How many others, she mused, would have given up long before this?

The descent continued and still, as Curtar pointed out to them, there was no sign of any life present on the planet when these upper rocks had been laid down. Then their companion did something with the lever and their downward motion slowed to a crawl. Finally, they stopped altogether.

Curtar pointed with his torch and said excitedly: "Now what do you see?"

Viona leaned over the rail, peering closely at the rock. There was a comparatively narrow demarcation line in the rock. Above it, there was nothing—but below it were what looked like bones clearly visible embedded in the solid rock.

"Notice how sharp and thin the demarcation line is between the empty stratum and the next?" Curtar exclaimed. "Whatever happened that brought the Deveranians to extinction must have occurred within an extremely short period. Either that—or they left this world en masse for some other planet but in all of my reading I can find no evidence at all for the latter."

He started the downward motion again and this time they went all the way down to the bottom of the tremendous shaft. Now the Amazon and Viona stared around them in genuine surprise. As Curtar opened the gate, they stepped into a huge cavern. Beside them, their guide flicked a switch and pointed towards a much shallower shaft. Three brilliant lights close to the ceiling illuminated everything and the Amazon recalled the thick cables, which she had first seen running up the wall towards the ancient spaceship.

"I've determined that what you see here represents the time when these people first came to this planet. You'll notice the smaller shaft yonder. There is no evidence of any life here below this level."

"And how long ago did all of this happen?" the Amazon queried.

"As near as I can determine—about three hundred thousand of your years after the galaxy was first formed. If I have interpreted the old writings accurately, that would be some time after this colony left their home planet, Derevan."

Closing the gate behind him, he went on, "Since I have no idea where Derevan is in the galaxy, or what form of propulsion their spacecraft used—whether or not they were aware of hyperspatial travel—I cannot say how long this journey took them. It may even be that they settled on other planets on their way here. There are so many variables that, at times, I feel I'm simply working in the darkness of total ignorance."

"Perhaps if we were to combine our scientific knowledge, we may be able to solve this problem." Already, the thought of finding the one planet in the entire galaxy where intelligent life began had taken a firm hold on the Amazon's scientific mind.

Switching off their torches, they walked forward. On the floor in the far corner were two complete skeletons. Examining them with a meticulous care, the Amazon finally straightened.

"From what I see here, it would appear that these creatures were winged."

Curtar nodded. "They were. This is why I'm positive that statuette is a true representation of them."

"Yet surely there's a contradiction here," Viona interposed. "If they were immortal, how is it that these bodies are here? It seems to me that they began to die not long after they arrived on this world."

"That's the only explanation I could reach," Curtar nodded in agreement, "that their immortality is somehow inextricably linked with conditions on Derevan. Here, and possibly on other planets if they stopped off on their way, the conditions were such that they lived long lives, perhaps a couple of centuries, but then died."

"Then it's possible they left Derevan searching for some other planet where the conditions were right for their continued immortality," Viona suggested. .

Curtar pursed his thin lips. "I can't argue with that."

He strode towards the far wall. "But this is what I really want you to look at." There was a small instrument standing on four thin rods near the wall. "You may recognize what this is," he went on.

"Of course." The Amazon gave a quick nod. "It's a highly sophisticated spectroscopic gravitometer."

"Exactly. There are three others covering this entire area, all accurately focused on one spot to give a three-dimensional image." From the table, he took three pairs of goggles, giving one to each of them. "Put these on and you'll then see what we have buried here."

Viona noticed there was a slender lead attached to the goggles and a moment later, he attached hers to the nearest gravitometer. Immediately, she staggered as the ground under her feet abruptly assumed a transparent, glassy look. For a moment she seemed to be standing on nothing. Putting out a hand, she held on to the chamber wall until her vision righted itself.

There was something buried not far below her—an oblong slab about seven feet long and three feet in width. By peering closely at it, she thought she could make out writing on the surface, but the image was not sharp enough to make out any of it.

"What is it?" she asked in a hushed tone.

"Some kind of obelisk," the Amazon answered. "Somehow, I doubt if it will be possible to read it like this. It will have to be completely excavated. Yet even if you get it out, it may not be a Rosetta Stone as you hope."

"Rosetta Stone?" There was a look of intense puzzlement on Curtar's grizzled features. "I don't understand."

The Amazon smiled. "The Rosetta Stone was a stone slab very much like this which was discovered on Earth, my home planet. It was engraved with a text given in three different languages. One—Greek—was well known whereas another, the ancient Egyptian hieroglyphics, some three thousand years old, had never been translated. This stone, however, enabled us to do that."

Viona removed her goggles, and everything returned to normal. "But that won't be possible in this case. From what you tell us, only the Derevanians ever lived on this world. There would be no other language they would translate theirs into."

"And as far as I'm aware, no other race came after them," Curtar interjected. "In all those millions of years since they became extinct, I'm quite sure I'm the first person to land here."

"Then I suggest we leave that to Abna once we get it out," the Amazon said with a trace of bitterness in her voice. She did not like to admit, even to herself, that his ability in this field of translating alien languages was in excess of her own.

Once back on the surface, they waited for the Ultra to return. An hour later, it landed smoothly close to where it had taken off. Abna came down the ladder and walked towards them.

"Well," the Amazon asked, "did you have any success?"

"There were no problems," he replied. "It wasn't difficult to locate Curtar's old site from his directions. As he said, there was plenty of copper ore there. Mexone and Thania are on board, smelting the pure metal. Soon, we'll have enough copper cubes to take us to the far end of the galaxy and back."

He threw a swift glance at Curtar standing a few feet away. For a moment there was an expression of suspicion on the aged features. Abna readily understood the reason for it. Since they were speaking in English, Curtar was still unsure of their motives.

"I think it might be better if I was to impress our language into Curtar's mind. It will make things a lot easier for us if we understand both languages and remove any doubts he might have if there is a two-way interchange of languages."

"That would be a good idea," the Amazon agreed. "Once you've done that, I'll let you know what's down there at the bottom of the shaft. It's truly amazing."

Abna walked towards Curtar. For an instant, the old man shrank away from the seven-foot giant standing over him as if fearing some form of attack. Smiling, Abna said quietly, using the Kezbekian tongue, "I'm not going to hurt you, Curtar. But so that you can fully believe we have no hostile intentions, I'm going to implant our language into your mind just as we learned yours."

Placing his hands gently on either side of the old man's head, he concentrated. Finally, he gave a brief nod. "There, it's done. Now we can all communicate in either language."

Turning to the Amazon, he went on, "You were going to tell me something about what you've found at the bottom of the shaft."

The Amazon nodded. "There's ample evidence that the Derevanians did once inhabit this planet. Curtar has already uncovered two complete skeletons."

Before she could go on, Viona interrupted excitedly, "There's also a huge slab buried just beneath the floor of the chamber. Curtar believes it's inscribed with the Derevanian script and he may be able to interpret most of it. All we have to do is get it out and bring it to the surface."

"That shouldn't be too much of a problem with the equipment we have on board the Ultra. I think we can make a quicker job of it than Curtar."

Abna was true to his word. Some four hours later, the obelisk had been carefully excavated and now saw the light of 'day' for the first time in billions of years. Between them, the Amazon and Abna carried it from the shaft into the building and placed it carefully onto the table.

Now, in the light they saw that it was not stone as they had first surmised but some kind of gray metal, much lighter than stone. Staring down at it, Curtar ran his fingertips over the inscribed characters with an almost loving reverence, an expression of sheer wonder on his aged face.

"This is something for which I've been searching for more than half of one of your centuries. There were times when I almost gave up the attempt but something made me continue."

"And you think you may be able to decipher it?" Thania asked.

"It will take time," the old man nodded and there was a smile on his lips. "But I believe so. Before I came here, I studied all there was to know of this race—and also a number of very ancient languages. It's possible that some of these are so old they may have been derived from that first language. If so, I may be able to do it by making certain correlations."

"If you need any help, I'll be glad to provide it," Abna said.

Leaving the old man poring over the ancient writing, the Cosmic Crusaders went outside into the eternal night of the planet. Overhead, the atmosphere was crystal clear.

On two sides the myriad stars of the Milky Way crowded across the heavens with the dark, mysterious Rift running in both directions between them. Here and there, narrower lanes of absorbing dust intruded upon the star fields like questing fingers of darkness.

After a short silence Viona asked, "Have you decided we should accompany Curtar on this quest for the primordial world, mother? It seems to me that we would be simply looking for the end of the rainbow."

Before the Amazon could reply, Mexone cut in. "After all, Amazon, we have no real evidence that this race still exists. It died out here. Who is to say that conditions on Derevan haven't altered drastically over a period of three or four billion years? What would be the use of simply looking for an old planet?"

"Furthermore," Abna said seriously, "there is one fact which we haven't considered. Here, we are talking about a race that came into existence some five or six billion years ago, long before Earth was even formed. In that time, the galaxy has rotated on its axis not once, but several times. Apart from a few suns close to the galactic center, all of the others have changed their original positions drastically. They are nowhere near the places they occupied when the Derevanians came into being."

"Perhaps you're right," the Amazon said coldly, "and I know that our main mission is to search out and help underdeveloped and oppressed races. But you are all putting forward arguments for not going on this mission. We are all scientists, brilliant scientists, and the literal meaning of the word 'scientist' is—a seeker after truth. Do none of you have any spark of imagination or scientific curiosity? Somewhere out there is the one unique planet in the entire galaxy and I say we should look for it."

"Evidently you've made up your mind, Vi," Abna replied, knowing it would be useless to argue with her. "So now everything rests on how far Curtar and I can get with that ancient alien language."

As things turned out, it was three days later before they made any breakthrough.

Working with the old man, Abna checked and rechecked their work. Since Curtar's knowledge was all based upon the Kezbekian grammar and scientific literature it was only logical that any translation would be made into his language.

Coming into the room, the Amazon went across to the table. Standing beside Abna she asked, "How is it going? Have you made any progress?"

Rubbing his eyes, Abna gave a slight nod. "I've been staring at these symbols for so long they now keep dancing in front of my vision. But—yes, we've made a little headway. This would seem to be a condensed history of their travels across the galaxy in search of other races and worlds which could be habitable for them."

He moved his hand slightly and indicated the curious array of dots at the bottom of the slab. "And we're pretty certain this is a star map and you'll see there are lines joining five of these dots."

"Then that must represent the journey this race took once they left Derevan." Viona's excited voice broke in on their conversation. Unnoticed, she had entered the room and was standing beside them. "The first and fifth dots are meant to be Derevan and this world and the three in between are the suns of the other planets they landed on during their journey here."

"A logical conclusion, Viona," Abna nodded. "But as yet we have no definite proof of that."

Curtar straightened, wincing as if the mere movement caused him pain. "Abna is being cautious," he said, running a hand down his cheek. "I myself am certain that we shall have translated all of this within the next few days."

The Amazon shot him a worried glance. "You seem to have something else on your mind, Curtar. For the past few days, you've spent almost every minute working with this script as if there isn't a moment to spare. What is it?"

The old man hesitated, then said soberly, "That vessel from Kezbek."

The Amazon frowned in puzzlement. "Surely there's nothing to fear from that now. I've no doubt it was destroyed by those missiles that Thania fired at it, otherwise it would have attempted another attack—and there's been nothing."

"That's true. But knowing my people, I'm quite sure that those on board that spaceship would have sent a message giving the exact whereabouts of this planet before you destroyed their spaceship. By now, others will be coming and this time there will be more of them."

"It's possible, Vi," Abna muttered gravely. "Perhaps we should have considered that possibility earlier." He turned to the old man. "How long will it take vessels from Kezbek to reach here?"

Pursing his lips, Curtar made a mental calculation before saying, "Approximately ten of your days if they left almost immediately on receiving that message."

"Then we don't have much time left," the Amazon agreed. "And neither of you have had more than a few hours sleep in the last three days. I'll fetch some restorative from the Ultra—but don't overdo it."

Over the next few hours, stimulated by the restorative, Abna and Curtar worked feverishly over the ancient characters. At the end of that time, they had succeeded in translating most of the message inscribed on the obelisk. A few symbols remained for which they could find no meaning and—much to Abna's disappointment—three of these were marked against the three suns on the star map that the Derevanians had visited during their long journey.

All of the Cosmic Crusaders were gathered in the room while Curtar read the transcribed record to them in a voice that trembled a little with subdued excitement.

"We of Derevan have long known that of all the many races which now live in the galaxy, we were the first. Once we attained the necessary scientific level we began to search for others, initially in our own region of space and then further afield until we had encompassed this whole galaxy of suns. We found nothing although there were many worlds that were evolving to the point where life could begin.

"Thus we began a program of ejecting life-spores into space knowing that in time, some would be drawn towards suitable worlds and thus life would begin. Alas, our experiment was only a partial success. Over more than a million years we watched as many races evolved to a high degree of scientific and cultural achievement and all eventually reached a point where they unlocked the secrets of the atom. They then had a choice—to venture out to the stars—or destroy themselves in a nuclear holocaust. Many fires were lit across the galaxy where entire worlds were destroyed in furnaces of atomic flame, leaving only dead cinders orbiting their parent suns.

"Only a small percentage had the wisdom to take the other path. Then a great catastrophe befell Derevan, a catastrophe so great that I will not write of this. However, terrible as it was for us, it provided the opportunity to search the various regions of space for the purpose of helping any of these races we might encounter to attain immortality as we had. We are one of those communities, our journey taking us across more than ninety thousand light years until finally we reached here only to discover that the race we hoped to find in this region had died out long before we arrived.

"Then a further disaster occurred. A cosmic storm of unprecedented violence struck the planet. It so affected our bodies that we became no longer immortal. Eventually, we too will become extinct but before that happens we are leaving behind this record in the hope that some race which is not motivated by greed and the lust for power may one day find it."

"So that's what happened to them once they landed here," the Amazon said somberly.

"A fitting testimonial to a noble race," Abna added.

"Now you're becoming sentimental," the Amazon retorted acidly. "It doesn't become you." She turned quickly. "I doubt if we'll learn much more from what lies at the bottom of that shaft, Curtar, and I think we can be fairly certain a fleet of spacecraft from Kezbek has already set out for this world. We now have to make a decision. Either we wait here until they come and make a fight of it—or we set out on one of the longest and strangest journeys the Ultra has ever made, tracing this route back to Derevan in the hope that we find it before the enemy does."

"So you intend to land on these three planets in turn and finally hope to discover Derevan?" Thania inquired.

"That's the general idea."

"Then since we have a rough idea of where Derevan lies—why don't we go there without wasting time on these three intermediate planets?" Mexone asked.

"Quite simply because we don't have sufficient copper to take us that tremendous distance in a single jump through hyperspace," the Amazon replied. "Furthermore, it would mean we would all be in a state of suspended animation for a much longer period than I think Curtar especially could withstand."

"Then since the Cosmic Crusaders is a democratic group, I suggest we put it to the vote," Viona said, "although I'm quite sure what the result will be."

CHAPTER IV

THE alien obelisk was quickly taken on board the Ultra and it was decided that Curtar should accompany them, leaving his own spacecraft behind on the planet. Although initially reluctant to follow this course, the Amazon had finally persuaded him that this was essential.

"The computer and drive we have on board the Ultra are far more advanced than yours," she explained. "For your vessel to approach light speed would take far too long to build up the required velocity and you would be unable to keep up with us. Furthermore, we have the means of entering the four-dimensional continuum at virtually any speed. It isn't necessary for us to attain a speed even close to light velocity."

"The other reason we're suggesting this," Abna told him persuasively, "is that with our super strength we can withstand the extreme acceleration needed. There will be no problem if you remain in one of the acceleration couches during that period of transition. You'll simply sleep through it."

So it was that the Ultra blasted off an hour later, cleaving swiftly through the atmosphere and into the darkness of the Cygnus Rift. While they increased velocity, Abna fed the information from the star map on the monument into the computer, also entering the time they estimated had elapsed since the pillar had been engraved.

"At the moment, I'm not sure how accurate the result will be," he said once the final batch of figures had been entered. "There are a lot of variables in these equations which are difficult to take into account."

"Since we've got the best computer there is, surely it's possible to figure out where this first star is from that map," Thania said. "The Derevanians would have made certain it's accurate."

"Of course they would. It would have been very accurate at the time they made that chart," the Amazon explained. "But not only is every star in the galaxy moving, the galaxy itself is revolving about its center. Over a period of a century, these movements don't make much of a change in the constellations you see from any world but in a billion years they amount to quite a lot. Most people on my own world are familiar with the constellations but I doubt if they would recognize them as they were a million years in the past or how they will look the same amount of time in the future."

Thania thought about that and then nodded. "I think I can understand that. So we may not even find this star once we get there."

"Once we get to within a few light years of our computed position, we'll try to refine our equations," Abna told her. "Right now, we'd better prepare ourselves for the jump into hyperspace. I would have preferred to travel through hyperspace in two stages owing to the tremendous distance to this first star on the chart and then get a better fix on it."

"Then why not do that?" Viona spoke up from the far end of the control console. "It makes sense."

"Unfortunately, using this ages-old star map, we can't pick a target star roughly midway between us and our objective. There are several marked, but the trouble is, in the interim, they will also have moved from their positions by unknown amounts. We'll just have to make it in one leap through hyperspace and hope for the best."

The Amazon moved towards the controls, resting her yellow fingers of the levers, setting them so that they could be operated by using the small secondary controls in the acceleration chamber.

Over her shoulder, she said, "You'd better get Curtar strapped down into one of the couches. I'm not certain how well he can withstand the acceleration towards near light velocity. After that, the computer will take over the controls."

In a compartment in the center of the huge vessel they all strapped themselves down onto the acceleration beds, with only their hands resting above the small banks of subsidiary controls, each linked to the master switches in the main control room.

Lying back, the Amazon closely watched the needle on the small screen raised over the couch so that, even lying flat, she could see it without difficulty. Smoothly, she increased the power in the engine matrix. Since the room was completely insulated, there was no sound to indicate that anything was happening. Her last glimpse of the screen showed the needle at just below light velocity.

The others, apart from Abna, lay quite still in their beds. He was still conscious and, turning his head, he flashed her a quick smile before they both slipped into the black oblivion of sleep.

Guided only by the faultless perfection of the electronic brains of the main computer, the Ultra reached its limiting velocity in normal space of just below light speed and was then suffused with the energy warp that injected it into the fourth dimension. Here the normal laws of velocity did not apply. Traveling at many times the speed of light the Ultra flashed through the galaxy. The pre-programmed electronic brains kept it on its predetermined course.

In the normal space-time continuum, light years fled by, tens and then hundreds of light years. Within the chamber, the Crusaders knew nothing of this. Then automatic relays responding to commands from the computer, clicked into place. The Ultra slipped out of the fourth dimension and back into normal space.

Hypodermic needles automatically injected each of them with a powerful restorative and a few moments later the Amazon stirred on her couch. The screen angled in front of her eyes told her they were no longer in hyperspace and that they had emerged with their original velocity—just a fraction below light speed.

Since there was now no acceleration or deceleration, they were all in a weightless condition. The Amazon flexed her shoulder muscles and then slid off the couch, holding tightly to a metal stanchion to prevent herself floating towards the ceiling. Swinging her way across the chamber, she snapped down a switch and a few seconds later, Earth-gravity returned.

By now the others were already stirring as consciousness returned. Curtar was the last to move. Grunting with the effort, he thrust himself onto his arms and stared about him. "Where are we— still in hyperspace?" he asked, forcing out the words with an obvious effort.

"No," the Amazon shook her head. "We emerged from hyperspace a few minutes ago." She threw a swift glance at the chronometer on the wall. "From our entry velocity and time in hyperspace, I'd say we've traveled some twenty thousand light years."

"Twenty thousand light years!" Curtar echoed the words as if he could not believe his ears. "Then we can't be far from the star marked on the chart."

"I suggest we remain here while we decelerate," the Amazon said briskly. She returned to her couch, clicked the strap and ran her slim hand over the subsidiary bank of controls and a moment later, the powerful retro rockets fired. The tremendous force thrust them forward against the straps. Breathing became difficult a conscious effort needed to force air in and out of their heaving lungs. Gradually, however, their tremendous forward velocity lessened until a needle on the small control panel told the Amazon they were now traveling at close on 50 thousand miles per hour.

"That should do it," she said tautly, cutting the rockets. "Now let's go along to the control room and take a look at exactly where we are."

The view from the huge observation window was disappointing. Staring out, Thania murmured, "There doesn't seem to be much to see. We appear to be in a very sparsely populated part of the galaxy."

A brilliant blue-white giant star blazed on the starboard bow and there were a few others in the vicinity—but nothing out of the ordinary as they had expected; nothing by which to choose any particular star from the others.

Abna walked forward, resting his hands on the control panel, allowing his keen gaze to wander over the view. Finally, he said, "There's a double star about thirty light years away."

"Perhaps we miscalculated how far stars have moved since the Derevanians left their world in this region," the Amazon suggested. "We could be dozens of light years from our objective."

Abna nodded. "Since we're dealing with such a tremendous period of elapsed time, I'd say that's quite likely."

"So, what do we do now?" Viona chipped in. "Carry out a sweep of the area?"

Seating himself in front of the controls, Abna sat in silence, gazing at the viewing screen, apparently lost in deep thought.

When he didn't speak for five minutes, the Amazon said tartly, "This is no time for just sitting around staring, Abna. We didn't come all this way just to look at the stars."

With a slight twist of his facial muscles, Abna said quietly, "I'm not just staring, Vi. I'm trying to put myself into the minds of the Derevanians. When they left their home-world all those billions of years ago, they stopped off at three stars on their journey to that sunless planet in the Cygnus Rift."

"We know that, father," Viona said.

"Yes, but my idea is that they wouldn't just choose three arbitrary planetary systems. I may be completely wrong, but I have the feeling that each system was very carefully chosen for some reason I can't quite fathom."

"Something which made them stand out from the thousands of others?"

"Exactly. If we can only figure out what it was, it may help us to locate this world even if it is now several light years away from its original place."

"There's one other thing which may provide us with a clue," Curtar said. He pointed towards the large obelisk. "I'll try to work out the meaning of that symbol next to this star. It must mean something important." He settled himself at the table where the obelisk lay, drawing up a chair and going through what they had already translated hoping to find something similar to the mysterious cipher.

Meanwhile, the Amazon seated herself in front of the screen connected to the 360-degree telescope, examining all of the stars within a three hundred light year radius of the Ultra.

"I hope we find something soon," Viona remarked. "Having nothing to do can be boring."

"Patience, daughter," the Amazon said, not once removing her gaze from the screen. "You need a lot of it when you're dealing with so many unknowns."

An hour passed in almost complete silence. Then Curtar pushed back his chair, rubbing his eyes.

"Find anything?" Abna asked, walking over.

"I'm not sure. There's nothing to which I can correlate this symbol with complete accuracy but the nearest I can get to it is 'veil'."

The Amazon swung round in her seat. Getting up, she motioned to Mexone to take her place and then walked to the table. "You think it may indicate a world—or sun perhaps—which is veiled in some way?"

Curtar shrugged. "That's as near a correlation as I can find. What it means, I'm not sure."

"It could possibly mean a planet with an exceptionally dense atmosphere," Thania conjectured.

"Or perhaps something like this." Mexone spoke suddenly from his position in front of the telescope controls, half-turning in his seat.

Almost as one, the others crowded around him. "There," he said with a trace of excitement in his voice. He pointed.

On the telescope screen where he indicated was an extremely faint, luminous object. It stood out from all of the other objects in the field of view. He turned a knob, slowly magnifying the image until it almost filled the small screen.

"It's a small veil nebula!" the Amazon exclaimed. "I think you've found the answer, Mexone. Can you give me an estimate of its distance?"

"I'd say about three hundred light years—give or take fifteen light years either way."

"Then that's what we aim for," she said briskly. "Work out the coordinates as accurately as you can. Once they're fed into the computer, we'll go back into hyperspace."

* * * *

This time when they slipped out of hyperspace, it was to view a sight like nothing they had encountered before. The electronic brains had already fired the retarding rockets and they were now decelerating, the velocity dropping towards a quarter light-speed.

Through the wide transparency of the viewing screen, they look upon a massive and intricate tracery of brilliant filaments of light. The entire screen was filled with them, a tangled silver braid enveloping several light years of space.

"I don't think I've ever seen anything so beautiful," Thania spoke up from a few feet away. "What are they?"

"They're the last remnants of a huge supernova which must have exploded several thousand years ago," Abna confirmed. "They're composed mainly of hydrogen and helium but with heavier elements in them which are all highly ionized. These excited atoms are responsible for the visible light."

The Amazon turned momentarily from the fantastic view outside. "It's believed that when the galaxy was very young a large number of super-massive stars were formed. Being so huge, they progressed through the stages of their evolution much more quickly than normal stars and ended their lives as super-supernovae. They were the first stars to synthesize the heavier elements in their interiors and then eject them into space. Without them, we would not be here since we, and everything upon which we exist, are made up of atoms formed in the interiors of those massive suns."

"And is it likely there can be any planetary systems here after such a catastrophic event?" Viona inquired.

"I'd say that's highly unlikely," Abna answered as the Amazon shot him a quick, questioning glance. "Unless there is such a sun which is the remnant of that tremendous detonation all those billions of years ago. If there is one I think it will be a highly peculiar star."

"Yes, father," Viona persisted. "But just think for a moment. If that is so, it fits in with these star charts made by the Derevanians. That sun they've marked along their journey must be one that stands out from the thousands of others in this region. What better way of standing out than to have been born of a super-supernova explosion?"

"The girl's right, of course," her mother declared emphatically. "I suggest we start looking for any stars in the vicinity of this nebula. But even if we find out, I think it highly improbable it will have any planets orbiting it." While the Amazon guided the Ultra through the wispy veils, the others sat at various instruments, scanning the region around them for any sign of a sun. For a time, it seemed that all of their efforts were in vain.

For all of them it was an eerie feeling, moving through a broad band of glowing gases and then entering the utter darkness of interstellar space which lay between the filaments, knowing that these were the result of that vast explosion which had, almost literally, blown a star to pieces at some time in the far distant past.

It was Curtar, standing next to the Amazon, who suddenly called out. "Are my old eyes deceiving me or can that be the star we're looking for—over on the starboard bow? It doesn't look like any star I've ever seen before."

The Amazon turned her head slightly from watching the instruments and followed his pointing finger. After a few moments of intense scrutiny, she said, "I think you're right, Curtar." Very slowly, she turned the nose of the mighty spaceship and watched as the object drifted across the viewing screen until it was in the exact center.

There, the wispy tendrils were less intense. Placing an arm around her shoulders, Abna leaned forward slightly, his brow creased in concentration. "Strange," he said softly. "It appears to be much smaller than Sol. In fact, I'd say it's not much larger than Earth."

"Why does that make it strange?" Thania inquired. "To me it looks just like an ordinary star even though it is extremely small."

Abna straightened. "It's strange because with a diameter as small as that, it's far brighter than it should be."

From behind them, Mexone said, "I've got an estimate of its distance, Amazon—less than two billion miles."

"As close as that?" For an instant there was disbelief in the Amazon's voice. "With such an obviously high temperature it should be a giant or supergiant star."

Abna studied it in puzzlement, then went back to check Mexone's figures. As he had expected, there was nothing wrong with them.

"A sun with a diameter only slightly more than that of Earth but as brilliant as a white giant sun." He seemed to be talking to himself. Then he gave a sudden nod. "Of course! That must be a white dwarf star out there. Certainly it seems strange even for these odd stars, but there's no other explanation."

"And what exactly is a white dwarf star?" Thania asked, ever anxious to learn something new.

"Almost certainly when that tremendously massive star exploded it ejected this nebula, glowing gaseous filaments which are the remains of much of its mass—but it left the core behind. There would be a massive explosive force acting outward but also an implosion in the center. This would compress the material of this star to a tremendous extent."

"That means," the Amazon interposed, "that a cubic inch of its material will weigh about as much as the Ultra. That gives you an idea of how dense it is. We'll also have to be prepared for its high gravitational field."

Spearing swiftly through the void, the Ultra headed for the strange sun. By the time it had swelled into an appreciable disc, they were close enough to search for any planets.

Not that any of them really expected to find any considering the way by which the white dwarf star had been formed in the middle of a truly titanic explosion.

Such indeed seemed to be the case. The tiny, tremendously dense sun now showed clearly on the viewing screen, an unblemished white surface devoid of any sign of sunspots.

Eyeing it closely, the Amazon said evenly, "If it continues along its normal course of evolution, that star will eventually become a neutron star. The force of gravity will crush all of the protons and electrons together and, depending upon its original mass, it may then become a black hole."

"All in all, a highly peculiar star," Mexone remarked. "However, it seems we're on a wild goose chase here unless the Deveranians came here while it was in the pre-supernova stage. It's possible there may have been planets at that time and they were all wiped out by that colossal explosion."

Abna nodded. "That would seem to be the logical conclusion, Mexone. I suggest we go on to that next star and—" He broke off sharply, then, "Hello, what's that just emerging from behind the sun?"

Leaning forward, resting her weight on her arms, the Amazon exclaimed. "It *is* a planet. It must have been occulted behind the sun. But surely that's impossible. How could it possibly have survived that detonation?"

There was a long silence as they turned this apparent paradox over in their minds.

Then Curtar said harshly, "The only explanation I can give is that this world entered this system some time after the star turned supernova."

After considering that possibility for a few moments, the Amazon turned and there was a strange expression in her violet eyes. "Then this must be more than a mere coincidence."

Mystified, Thania asked, "What coincidence, Amazon?"

"Don't you see?" There was a trace of exasperation in the Amazon's voice as she stared at their puzzled faces. "First we land on a planet wandering free in the Cygnus Dark Rift without an attendant sun. Here we come across another planet which must have been drifting alone through space before being captured by this star."

"You're right as usual, Vi," Abna admitted. "But surely you're not suggesting that these two worlds had a common origin? After all, they're at least twenty thousand light years apart. That would be stretching coincidence a little too far for me."

Viona spoke up, brushing a strand of her copper-colored hair from her forehead. "I think we should first land on that world and satisfy ourselves that the Derevanians did come here. At the moment, we can't be absolutely certain."

"Just what I was going to suggest," the Amazon said, nodding.

CHAPTER V

WITH the Amazon at the controls, the Ultra entered a cruising orbit ten thousand miles above the mystery planet. At the controls, Abna checked the data that came up on the analyzer.

"Diameter roughly that of Earth," he said. "Atmosphere very similar but with more water vapor which indicates a high humidity. The overall temperature varies from 50 degrees at the equator to 20 degrees at the polar regions which would account for the absence of any ice caps."

Seated in front of the telescope screen, Viona added further details. "There's quite a lot of thick cloud down there obscuring large areas of the surface. However, I can make out two large oceans, numerous rivers, but much of the equatorial region is desert. The rest would appear to be covered by dense forest. No sign of any cities or towns—in fact, no indication at all of intelligent life." She added the last as a disappointed afterthought.

The Amazon's agile brain had already assimilated everything. Smoothly, she piloted the Ultra down through the atmosphere. As they dropped lower the cloud layer thickened. Reaching out a yellow hand, she snapped down the switch of the radar equipment. Instantly, details appeared on the small subsidiary screen to her left providing her with accurate estimates of their varying altitude.

She had already decided to land the Ultra at a spot where the equatorial desert met the jungle region, thereby giving them the opportunity to examine these two different regions together.

The Ultra landed with scarcely a bump on soft sand. Silence enclosed the vessel as she switched off the mighty engines.

"Now let's see what we've got here," she said briskly, getting lithely to her feet. "It's time we did some exploring."

"You mean we go out there to look for any evidence that the Deveranians ever landed here?" Abna put in.

"That's the reason we crossed twenty thousand light years," she answered. "From our observations I doubt if we'll need our suits but the heat and humidity are going to present a problem."

Making their way to the airlock, Abna pressed the button which operated the mechanism and they waited until it had swung open to its fullest extent and the retractable ladder had descended to the ground thirty feet below. The air that swept in through the opening held a burning touch and immediately brought the sweat out on their faces and bodies in spite of their light clothing.

Viona was the first out, clambering swiftly down the ladder, dropping the last five feet onto the soft sand. The others quickly followed. The intense heat hit them at once and it took a little while for their breathing to adjust to the hot, dry air.

Around them, on three sides, the ochre sand stretched away to every horizon. About a mile away however, towards what they believed to be the north, a line of dense white fog hid everything in that direction.

Viona eyed it in obvious puzzlement. "What can that be?" she asked, pointing.

Surveying it with a keen gaze, the Amazon finally replied, "My guess is that it marks a dividing line between the desert and the cooler jungle. Condensation of the moist air meeting the heat of this desert would account for the fog."

"Account for the fog—yes," Abna said, "but not for such a narrow demarcation line between the two. It's almost as if there's never been any thermal equilibrium between these two regions. There has to be some form of air movement, some mixing of hot and cooler air. It doesn't make sense. The laws of thermodynamics state that heat will flow from a hot to a cooler region until they're in a state of equilibrium."

"Then I reckon we should make for that fog and see just what is going on. As far as I can see there's nothing but sand in this desert and—" The Amazon broke off at a sudden movement about half a mile away to their left.

The sand suddenly emptied into a huge fountain of yellow. A huge scaly head on top of a long sinewy neck reared high into the shimmering air.

"What under the stars is that?" Thania yelled. She pulled her disintegrator from her belt, gripping it tightly in her right hand.

Swiftly, the others did likewise. Peering into the glaring brilliance the Amazon muttered, "It would seem this desert isn't quite as empty as it looks."

The massive head turned in their direction. A gigantic mouth opened revealing long rows of teeth. Acid saliva dripped onto the sand. Then, with a booming roar it came towards them, lifting a bow wave of sand in front of it. While it was still some distance from them, a second creature appeared—and then a third!

With a wild yell, Curtar turned and began running towards the fog bank at their backs, his feet sliding and slipping in the treacherous sand.

Tensely, the Cosmic Crusaders stood their ground until the creatures came within killing range of their weapons. Aiming for the head of the first monster, the Amazon squeezed the stud. The pencil beam of energy hit the creature just below the right eye.

Large chunks of scaled flesh disintegrated.

Sand erupted and boiled as the creature shuddered in its death throes. The whirling cloud threw it straight into their eyes, temporarily blinding them. By the time they managed to wipe the grains from their eyes and were able to see again, the remaining two sand-monsters were almost upon them. Abna swung sharply as one of the creatures somehow turned swiftly in a half-circle, hoping to come upon them from behind.

The disintegrator beam struck the weaving neck halfway along its tremendous length. Hot ichor spouted from the wound onto the sand but in spite of the terrible wound, the creature was somehow still alive and dangerous. The gaping maw swept down towards him, seeking to grip him around the waist and tear him in half.

Before it could do so, however, the Amazon had leapt forward, dropping her weapon for fear of hitting her husband. Her arms reached out, grasping two of the enormous incisors in each hand. Gritting her teeth, she exerted all of her superhuman strength, forcing the monster's jaws apart. Muscles stood out along her arms as she pulled the jaws further and further apart, bracing herself on the precariously shifting sand as the sand-creature tried desperately to pull away.

Then the hideous head fell away. Panting a little with the exertion, she glanced quickly around to find that both Viona and Mexone had fired death-dealing shots into the massive body just showing above the sand. The third creature was lying a short distance away, its lidless eyes slowly glazing over.

"Thanks, Vi," Abna gave an appreciative nod. "That was a near thing."

The Amazon flashed him a quick smile. "I couldn't let that thing have you for its breakfast." She then became more serious. "I think we should try to find Curtar. He seems to have vanished into that fog. This desert is a little too dangerous."

A few feet away, Thania stared wide-eyed at the huge bodies. Twisting her lips into a wry grimace, she said, "Something tells me that the jungle yonder may have even more unpleasant surprises in store for us."

"There's only one way to find out," the Amazon replied. "We also have to reach Curtar before he runs into more trouble than he can handle."

Cautiously, they approached the high wall of white fog. It was so dense and rose so high that it blotted out everything that lay on the other side. Giving it a penetrating glance, Abna said tautly, "I suggest we all stick very close together. We don't know how far it extends and we could easily lose each other."

Holding their weapons ready, they entered it and immediately felt the abrupt drop in temperature. Advancing in a line, it was impossible for any of them to see further than the two immediately beside them. Thick and cloying, it hung unmoving around them, touching their exposed flesh with clammy fingers, soaking into their clothing until they seemed saturated with it.

"This is unlike anything I've come across before." Mexone's voice seemed oddly muffled. "But you were right, Abna, about there being some strangely stable demarcation line of temperature here. It must have dropped some 30 degrees in the space of a couple of feet."

"Then either the laws of thermodynamics as we know them don't apply here or there are some highly peculiar forces at work on this world," Abna answered. "But unless this fog ends soon we could find ourselves wandering around in circles." Raising his voice, he shouted, "Curtar! Where are you?"

There was no answer. Either the old man was much further away than they had thought or the mist was such that even his shout was deadened to the point where his voice was unable to penetrate far.

For what seemed ages, they shuffled forward, always keeping in sight of each other. At times strange swirling vortices appeared like miniature tornados, disappearing just as quickly. Then, with an abruptness that took them all by surprise, the fog ended. Behind them, stretching away on either side was the thick wall of white. In front of them were gigantic jungle trees draped with loops of thick, fernlike creepers.

Now they were in the open, Abna called Curtar's name again and this time a faint echo came from somewhere to their left. It echoed eerily among the trees so that it was impossible for them to gauge the direction accurately.

The Amazon pointed. "I suggest we spread out and look for him. But don't go too far. It will be just as easy to lose ourselves in this vegetation as in that mist back there."

Moving away to the right of the others, Viona adjusted the beam of her disintegrator, slowly cutting a path through the intense tangle of growths that confronted her. It was slow work and, glancing behind her, she noticed to her horror that already new life was springing up, emerging from the blackened earth.

But there was no turning back now. She could pick out the shouts of the others as they forged on into the teeming jungle. Lifted her head, she called loudly. "Curtar! Where are you?"

This time a shout came from somewhere close by just ahead of her. Desperately, she cut her way forward and a few minutes later was astonished to find no tall growths in front of her, barring her way. She had stumbled into a wide clearing covered in a carpet of gray moss. Curtar was there, standing absolutely still in the center, staring wildly about him.

Holstering her gun, she walked up to him. His back was to her now and he whirled swiftly at her soft approach. Then an expression of utter relief crossed his grizzled features.

"Everything's all right, Curtar," she told him. "I'll call the others."

Five minutes later they were all assembled in the glade. Moistening his thin lips, the old man stuttered, "What...what were those creatures in the desert. I thought you'd all been killed."

Smiling slightly, the Amazon replied, "It would take more than three of those sand-monsters to kill us." She made to say something more; then held up her hand for silence.

After a few moments, Thania whispered, "What is it, Amazon? Do you hear something?"

"There's something here. I'm sure of it."

"Funny, I've had the feel of eyes on the back of my neck ever since we came into this jungle," Abna confirmed.

Meticulously, he studied the trees and undergrowth all around them, his keen gazed missing nothing. "I don't see anything."

The attack came without warning and from a direction they had not expected. One moment there was utter silence. The next second, dark hairy shapes dropped from the topmost branches of the surrounding trees. They had glimpses of squat, black bodies and brutish faces. Abna and Viona both fired in almost the same instant and two of the brutes went down.

A third dropped onto the Amazon's shoulders, clearly hoping to pin her to the ground beneath its tremendous weight. Both Mexone and Thania yelled a sudden warning—but it was not needed. The Amazon had seen the danger but made no attempt to avoid it. Her knees bent slightly under the impact. Then, in a single fluid movement, she straightened her legs, balancing the huge creature across her shoulders. The brute emitted a grunt of what might have been surprise that somehow, this slender woman had not collapsed under its far superior weight.

The next moment, she got her hands under it, lifting it high above her head. For a few moments, she held it there. Then, with a slight twist of her waist, she hurried the ungainly body at the nearest tree. The creature struck the trunk with bone-shattering force, hung there momentarily, and then slid inertly to the ground.

But there were still several more of the brutes to contend with. With so many milling around in the clearing it soon became apparent that the disintegrators were just as much a danger to themselves as to the enemy. Swiftly, Mexone pulled a long-bladed knife from his belt, urging the others to do likewise.

Another hairy creature dropped from the overhead branches and landed directly in front of him. Long arms caught him around the middle, pulling tighter. Acting purely by instinct, he hauled his right arm free of the creature's bone-cracking embrace. The razor-sharp edge of the knife sliced across his adversary's throat in a single movement. Spurting blood, the creature reeled back, slumping to its knees.

Another had grabbed Viona from behind, pinning her arms to her sides. She reacted swiftly. Bending backward, she lifted her feet from the ground; tensed her iron muscles and then pulled herself forward with a mighty heave, throwing the monster over her shoulders. Before it could regain its feet, her knife slid between its ribs.

Ten minutes later it was all over. Eight grotesque bodies lay strewn about the clearing.

The remainder had fled, leaping up into the branches. The sound of their retreat died slowly away.

"What kind of monsters are these?" Thania asked a trifle breathlessly.

Staring down at the brutish features of the nearest creature, the Amazon remarked,

"Evidently some species near the bottom of the evolutionary ladder."

Abna nodded. "Which makes me think that this is not the planet the Deveranians visited during their journey through space. These brutes, those monsters in the desert—and all of this lush, primal vegetations suggests this is a young planet."

"Perhaps," the Amazon said musingly. "I think we have to find out more about it before we can be sure on that point."

Abna regarded her studiously for a moment. "What makes you so uncertain, Vi?"

"One thing we did not see during our aerial survey and there's been no evidence of it since we landed."

"What's that?" Viona asked.

"Isn't it obvious? Volcanic activity. All of the theories of planetary formation, especially those like this, which are clearly Earth-type worlds, require an early period of intense vulcanism during their evolution. In spite of all we've seen that makes me sure that this is an old planet, possibly even older than Earth."

"Then the only way we can prove that is to find some evidence that the Derevanians actually did land here some billions of years ago." Mexone said.

"Perhaps if we were to follow that path yonder it might lead us somewhere." Viona pointed towards what they had earlier surmised was merely a gap in the trees.

That it was indeed a path was soon evident. Judging by its width, a little over two feet, it had certainly not been made by some large animal. Nor, as the Amazon pointed out, was it likely to have been made by those creatures that had attacked them since their mode of travel appeared to be through the upper branches of the jungle.

Moving cautiously in a single file, they thrust their way through tangling creepers with stalks like steel wire. Long ropelike strands hung across the track at intervals adding to their difficulties. Then, after an hour of progress they heard a sound coming from the distance ahead.

"What is it?" Thania asked in a hushed whisper. "It sounds like a lot of voices all chanting together."

"That's just what it is," Abna said, after listening intently for a few moments. "I think we're going to meet some of the natives of this world." Throwing a meaningful glance in the Amazon's direction, he added, "I don't think we're going to find anyone of a reasonably high intelligence."

They thrust their way through a dense cluster of bushes, their large, spatulate leaves forming a screen through which it was impossible to see anything. Aiming her disintegrator, the Amazon cut a foot-wide gap through the wall of green. Peering through it, they stared at an incredible scene.

A large clearing lay in front of them with a high wall of rock to their right. The smooth surface was embossed with weird, outlandish figures interspersed with rounded columns as high as the rock-face between them. Once those columns had been highly polished but now they were scored and pitted by long ages of wind and rain.

Almost filling the open space was a horde of natives, all on their knees with heads bowed until their foreheads were touching the ground. But it was not these that caught, and held, the undivided attention of the Crusaders.

Directly in front of a huge hemispherical opening in the rock stood a huge statue and, for the watchers, there was no mistaking what it was—the strange, almost birdlike, features and the great wings outspread.

"That's a statue of a Derevanian," Viona gasped in awed amazement. "Then we must be on the right track. But why are those natives bowing down to it?"

"Perhaps they believe it's their god," Mexone whispered.

The Amazon shook her head. "Not that exactly," she murmured thoughtfully. "Take a closer look at those natives and you'll see what I mean."

Switching their gaze from the awesome idol, the others ran their gaze over the mass of bowed figures. It was Viona who put their thoughts into words. "Their features have a similar look to that statue and there are vestigial wings sprouting from their shoulders."

"Exactly." The Amazon spoke with a trace of satisfaction in her voice. "This is an old world and here we have a case of reverse evolution. The progenitors of these natives were the original Derevanians who came here billions of years ago. Some time ago they must have reached a point in their evolution where they could go no further and now they've devolved into these pitiful, pathetic creatures."

"I guess you're right, Vi," Abna admitted. "That being the case, it's clear that everything on this world also entered a state of retrograde evolution, reverting back to the prehistoric age we see now."

He pointed towards the ancient embossing. "That must be some kind of temple. I'd certainly like to have a look inside. It's just possible there may be some incredibly ancient records there which may help us locate the next star."

"No sooner said than done," the Amazon replied. Drawing herself up to her full height, she pushed through the vegetation and strode into the clearing. She was spotted almost immediately. With a single yell, the natives rose to their feet, turning to stare at the intruder.

For a moment, there was indecision on their faces. Then they turned to make a concerted run at her. Instantly, she lifted the disintegrator in her hand, aimed it at the rock-face some distance from the entrance and pressed the stud. A huge chunk of stone blasted into the air. Moving her hand slightly, she repeated the process but this time aiming just in front of the nearest line of natives. The beam scored a deep furrow in the ground.

For a moment, they stood there in shocked amazement. Then, as one man, they turned and ran, pouring in a dark tide into the jungle some four hundred yards away.

Lowering the weapon, the Amazon said thinly, "There, I think we've seen the last of them for the time being." Glancing at Mexone and Viona, she said, "Keep a close watch just in case they do pluck up enough courage to return."

Motioning to Curtar to accompany them she led the way with Abna and Thania close behind.

There was plenty of light inside the temple. The brilliant white light from the slowly setting white dwarf sun glared through the opening highlighting every detail. Everywhere were strange objects at whose nature it was impossible for them to make even a reasoned guess. Most of them were corroded and falling to pieces.

At the far side was a long oblong block of black stone adorned with strange figuring.

Curtar immediately darted forward, his movements extremely agile for a man of his age.

He stood in front of the stone, gripping it tightly with his hands, an expression of rapt wonder on his wrinkled features.

As the others came up to him, he reached out his hand, moving it almost reverently across the smooth surface. What happened next was something none of them expected.

As his hand brushed against an almost invisible projection, there was a loud click and a segment of the stone on top slid noiselessly aside. It revealed a deep cavity some four feet square.

The old man made to put his hand inside, but the Amazon grabbed his wrist. "Be careful," she said warningly. "That could be a trap of some kind."

Releasing him, she placed both hands flat on the edge of the stone and with a powerful push of her legs, swung herself on top of the block. Slowly, she edged her way across it; then took a small but powerful torch from her belt. Switching it on, she shone the beam inside the aperture.

"Can you see anything?" Thania asked.

The Amazon nodded without replying. Reaching one hand inside the cavity, she drew out something that shone brilliantly in the light.

Easing herself to the edge of the slab, she dropped lightly to the floor, the others crowding around her, peering at the object she held.

It was a highly polished metal plate. At first sight, it appeared to be completely blank but a close scrutiny showed that it was inscribed with tiny characters, so small they were scarcely visible to the naked eye.

Holding the plate in front of Curtar, tilted slightly so that the light struck obliquely across it, the Amazon asked, "Do these look like those Derevanian characters on the block you found?"

After a brief scrutiny, the old man said, "They are certainly very similar." He remained silent for a moment; then uttered a sudden cry of astonishment. "Look! Here at the very bottom. A diagram almost exactly the same as the others but now with four stars joined. I think this tells us we're definitely on the right track for Derevan."

CHAPTER VI

THE journey back through the jungle was more enervating than their previous trek. True the brilliant white sun was setting, dropping ever closer to the unseen horizon, but the coming of twilight brought out all kinds of flying insects, much larger than normal, some with wicked looking stings in their tails. Eventually, however, just as the light was beginning to fade, they passed through the clearing where they had encountered the tree-living creatures.

There was no sign of any bodies now. Clearly, while they had been gone, more of the monsters had returned and taken their dead away. Ten minutes later, they came upon the fog. Now it seemed even thicker than before, clogging their throats and hampering their breathing. Keeping closely together, holding on to each other, they passed through it.

In front of them lay the desert, countless miles of sand—but there was no sign of the Ultra!

All of them stared in stunned surprise, disbelieving eyes searching every inch of the ground. It was Viona who said, "This must be the place where we landed. I'm sure that was the same clearing even though there were no bodies left."

"I can't believe it!" Thania exclaimed. "It's impossible for the Ultra to disappear like that. None of the creatures on this planet are capable of operating it."

"We left the airlock open," Mexone reminded them as they hurried across the sand.

Fifteen minutes they reached the deep indentation in the sand where the Ultra had landed.

Apart from that, and the trail of their own prints leading towards the jungle, there was no evidence the spaceship had ever been there.

The Amazon turned to speak with Curtar but the old man was now some distance away. A moment later, he raised his hand and shouted. Hurrying to him, they saw what he had discovered—a second deep, circular depression.

"There's been another spaceship here," Curtar muttered. "It would not surprise me if it was a Kezbekian ship. Somehow, they must have followed us to this planet. Look! There are other prints in the sand heading towards where the Ultra stood."

"But how could they have known about this star?" Viona interrupted.

"That will have to wait," the Amazon snapped thinly. "Now we have to think quickly and logically. If there was another vessel and they have taken the Ultra, it's possible we wouldn't have heard either the landing or the take-off because of that muffling effect of the fog. But somehow, we have to—" She broke off quickly, staring at Viona, her violet eyes wide.

"Viona! You're still wearing that Daranian teleporter belt you took from that alien in that strange artificial multiple sun system we last visited."

"I know," the girl replied, still puzzled by her mother's remark. "I often slip it on. It means I then have teleportation powers just like father's only he doesn't need anything like this. But how does this help?"

"Don't you see? If the Ultra hasn't slipped into hyperspace—and it's possible they haven't got the know-how to operate those special controls—there might just be a chance we can get it back."

"What exactly are you suggesting, Vi?" Abna asked.

"Our daughter knows how to use that belt. All she has to do is visualize in her mind the control room of the Ultra, then flick that switch and if the ship isn't too far away—or in hyperspace—she'll be teleported there. And if you and I clasp her arms tightly, we'll go with her. That's how it happened on Zerzura when they kidnapped her." She handed the shiny metal plate inscribed with the Derevanian characters to Mexone.

"You remain here with Thania. If we're successful, it won't be long before we return for you. And keep a look out for those natives."

"I suppose this method might just be possible," her husband conceded. "A lot will depend upon how far the Ultra is now. We don't know the maximum range of that belt."

"Stop pussyfooting around, Abna. We'll just have to make the attempt. It's the only chance we have and the longer we stand here discussing possibilities and probabilities, the further the Ultra will be from us."

"I'm willing to try," Viona said stoutly.

Grasping the girl's arms and holding their weapons in their free hands, they waited tensely as Viona concentrated on the familiar interior of the Ultra's control room.

Just before she reached for the switch, the Amazon said with a touch of steel in her voice, "Once we get there, dive in three directions and kill anything that moves."

Viona flicked down the switch. There was an instant of blackness too short to be taken in fully and then the glare of light in their eyes. Blinking the Amazon flung herself sideways and down, hitting the floor and rolling over on her right shoulder jerking up her protonic gun, her keen gaze taking in everything in a single moment.

Two men stood at the control panel, their backs to her. Two others stood close to the armament controls on either side of the room while a fifth was standing less than three feet from where the trio had abruptly materialized. She almost laughed at the expression of stupefied amazement on his hard features.

He recovered himself instantly, uttering a strangled yell. His right hand dropped towards his waist just as the beam from the Amazon's gun sliced across his chest pitching backward. He crashed onto the floor without a further sound.

The two men bending over the controls had half-turned when the twin beams from Abna's and Viona's weapons hit them. Reeling drunkenly, they both fell sideways across the controls before sliding inertly onto the floor.

A heat beam sizzled through the air just above the Amazon's head as one of the Kezbekians at the side of the cabin managed to get off a shot. The next moment, the Ultra lurched violently. Acceleration abruptly threw them across the room, slamming them against the rear wall with stunning force. All three blacked out momentarily but their superhuman strength somehow saved them from injury.

The remaining Kezbekians had not been so fortunate. One lay with his neck broken against a metal stanchion, his blaster still in his hand. The second had somehow managed to save himself from serious injury. Now he was on his feet, struggling forward against the savage acceleration, using his left hand to raise his other arm that held his gun.

Somehow, Viona found the strength to lunge forward, bent almost double. Her head slammed into the Kezbekian's stomach. Gripping him tightly around the waist, her arms pinning his to his side, she thrust him back against the hull. Exerting all of his strength, he tried to push the slim girl away, but his muscles were no match for Viona's.

Straightening up, she lifted him from the floor and then, with a swift backward bend, she heaved him over her head sending him spinning across the floor. Before he could get up, Abna turned. The beam from his blaster took the man full in the chest.

The Amazon gave him only a cursory glance before thrusting herself steadily towards the controls. Abna caught her arm to help her but she shook is hand away.

Together they finally made it. Hauling the dead enemy away, they stared down at the mass of levers and switches.

Clenching his teeth, Abna said, "One of them evidently fell across the acceleration lever when he died. We're now streaking out into spaced at close to light velocity."

Without answering, the Amazon ran her tawny fingers over the switches and levers, diverting the power into the retro rockets. Slowly, the red needle on the dial began to creep back as their tremendous speed diminished.

Once she had reduced their velocity to a suitable speed, she turned the nose of the Ultra in a wide arc until they were facing back the way they had come. Fortunately, there was no difficulty in determining the position of their objective. The huge veil nebula was still clearly visible on the screen stretching across several light years of space.

Relaxing a little, the Amazon remarked. "Well, at least our plan worked, and we've regained control of the Ultra."

"So now we head back to that planet and pick up the others," Viona said. "Then we just—"

She broke off in mid-sentence. Pointing, she cried, "The Derevanian obelisk! It's gone!"

During the brief battle, they had not given any attention to the table that had held the obelisk.

Grimly, Abna said, "There's no doubt the Kezbekians must have taken it with them. That means if they can decipher any of that language and realize the meaning of those dots at the bottom, they'll know the route the Derevanians took."

"And they have a head start on us," the Amazon muttered harshly. "There's no time to be lost. We must get the others and then head for the next star. At least we'll have that inscribed plate to help us and if that map is more accurate than the other, we may still get there first. I don't doubt we have the better and faster spacecraft."

* * * *

Now there was nothing for Mexone, Thania and Durvan to do but wait. All three were aware that their present situation was precarious to say the least. On one side of them stretched the seemingly innocuous desert, a vast expanse of ochre sand—but one that, as they had discovered, contained those enormous snakelike creatures.

On the other side of them was that great wall of thick fog—and behind that were other equally dangerous denizens of this world—as well as those natives. At any time they might decide to trail them. Every member of the Cosmic Crusaders was well aware that the strange metal plate that Mexone now gripped tightly in his hands was also certainly something regarded as sacred by those degenerate descendants of the original Deveranians. It would not be long before they decided to try to get it back.

With the white sun now dropping swiftly out of sight, a bitterly cold wind got up, swirling around the trio in savage gusts that chilled them to the bone. Shivering, the teenager lay back on the sand that still held some of the terrific heat of the day. Reaching into her pouch she took out some of the food she had brought with her, handing some to Mexone and Curtar.

Chewing reflectively on it, she said between mouthfuls, "Do you think the Amazon and the others managed to reach the Ultra, Mexone?"

"We can only hope so. Even though Abna tried to explain it once, I've really no idea how those belts work. It's possible they have a safety device built into them to prevent the wearer emerging into empty space—since without a spacesuit that would mean death within seconds. My guess is that if the wearer did materialize in empty space, the belt would instantly return him to the point where he started."

"And since that obviously hasn't happened," Curtar put in, "I think we can assume they reached the Ultra safely."

"I'm sure the Amazon would have taken such a possibility into account before they left." Thania tried to force conviction into her voice.

A quarter of an hour passed with only a contemplative silence among them. Then a sudden sound disturbed the stillness. It was a thunderous thudding that came from just behind them.

Instantly, they leapt to their feet, hands reaching for their weapons. The noise increased in violence. The mist was closing behind something huge that had emerged into the dusk. For a stunned moment, they stared at it. They had seen some large animals before but this thing was monstrous.

Like some terrifying armadillo it came out into the open. A massive plated carapace covered much of its body from which protruded a fearsome head on a short thick neck.

Two large tusks jutted from its lower jaw. It must have weighed more than a hundred tons and its short legs, each bearing a long forward-pointing spike, carried it forward at a slow, but frightening, pace.

Once completely in the open it uttered an ear-splitting roar. There was no doubt it had seen the duo for the next moment it started towards them, moving awkwardly but with a grim and deadly purpose. Swiftly, both aimed their disintegrators and fired. Instantly, the head and neck disappeared beneath the shell as chunks of it flew in all directions—but it was clear the monster felt little of any damage their rays caused. Beneath that massive protective covering, it was almost impossible for them to hit any part of its body.

"Your weapons don't seem to be having any effect," Curtar called urgently. "What do we do now?"

Staring wildly about him, Mexone saw their only chance. "Run into the desert!" he replied. "Quickly!" He grasped Thania's hand and pulled her along. Curtar followed, pushing himself to the limit of his strength.

Without thinking, Thania raced beside Mexone across the yielding sand. She couldn't imagine what they would gain by this maneuver but clearly Mexone had some plan in mind. The three of them ran full tilt for a hundred yards; then stopped. Wonderingly, Thania turned and stared behind her expecting to find the beast close on her heels.

Instead, its momentum was carrying it slowly forward but its tremendous weight was causing it to sink deeply into the yielding sand.

Further and further it slid, as the desert gave way beneath its enormous bulk. Emitting roar after roar, it was soon almost totally submerged. As they watched, it slowly disappeared from sight. Sand cascaded into the gaping hole, covering the creature completely. A few minutes later, it was impossible to make out where it had been.

Thania let her breath go in a long, relieved sigh. But they were not finished with trouble yet. Glancing up from the spot where the creature had vanished, Mexone said tautly, "It looks as though we're still not in the clear."

Night had now fallen but the brilliant light from the glowing filaments almost filling the entire sky showed them the dark horde that now came pouring out of the mist. Almost fifty of the natives, most brandishing primitive weapons, came charging towards them. A thrown spear half buried itself a foot from where Curtar was standing. More came arcing through the air.

Swiftly, Mexone aimed his gun. Keeping his thumb on the stud, he slowly swung it in a wide arc. Several of the enemy went down, dropping to the sand without a sound. Thania joined in and more died. The rest now halted uncertainly, evidently surprised by the destructive power of the disintegrators. Withdrawing a short distance, they began jabbering animatedly among themselves.

"Evidently they didn't expect to find that we can take good care of ourselves," Thania said. "But they don't seem to be intent on leaving."

"They clearly want this plate back and they'll do anything to get it no matter how many of them are killed in the attempt," Mexone answered grimly.

"What are they doing now?" The teenager pointed.

Several of the natives were moving back towards the fog. A moment later they vanished into it leaving only a small group behind.

"They've probably gone to collect reinforcements," Curtar suggested.

When the natives made no further attempt to attack there was nothing the trio could do but await events. These were not long in forthcoming. Something emerged from the fog, something dark and large. Several moments fled before the duo recognized what it was—a large wooden structure with a metal shield at the front.

At first, Mexone thought it was set on wheels but then he noticed it slid forward on flat wooden runners so as not to sink into the soft sand. Moving quickly, the natives hid themselves behind it, helping the other to thrust it forward.

"It seems they mean business this time, Thania," he muttered grimly, lifting his blaster. He squeezed the stud twice, sending the energy beam directly at the protective shield. To his surprise, the ray merely bounced off the palely shining surface.

"The disintegrators are useless against that metal," Thania cried, "and being on runners it won't sink like that monster."

"Then there's nothing we can—" Mexone never finished his sentence. There was a mighty roar that seemed to shake the entire planet to its core. A sizzling beam of energy came from somewhere above them. It struck the natives and the odd machine in a blaze of light. When the three could see again, the enemy was gone and the Ultra was screaming overhead as it turned and prepared to make a landing.

* * * *

Safely back on board the Ultra, they watched as the strange world dropped away into the void until its white dwarf sun was no longer distinguishable from the surrounding nebula. Briefly, the Amazon told them what had happened once they had found themselves back on board the spaceship, how the Kezbekians had taken the stone obelisk and were now almost certainly in hyperspace, heading for the next star marked on the Derevanian chart.

Curtar's extreme disappointment showed clearly on his grizzled features as he heard this news but cheered up slightly as Mexone handed him the inscribed plate. Drawing a chair up to the table, he studied it meticulously through the powerful magnifying glass that Abna gave him.

After a few minutes, he glanced up, a frown creasing his brow. "This is undoubtedly written in the Derevanian language but unless my memory deceives me, this star map is slightly different from that on the obelisk."

"Why should that surprise you?" the Amazon asked. "It was obviously made long before the other and that star in the Cygnus Rift won't be marked on it."

"No, it's not that." Curtar shook his head emphatically. "There's something else. That sun which they left before coming here is in a slightly different position and here it's marked as a double star!"

"You're sure of that?" The Amazon took the magnifying glass from him and peered intently at the inscribed dots. Then she looked up and smiled at Abna standing close beside her. "He's right. Take a look for yourself and if I remember rightly, the symbol next to it is also not the same as that on the pillar."

"Then we may still have a chance of beating those others to the Derevanian's stopping off planet—even if they are now in hyperspace."

"It certainly looks like it," the Amazon agreed. Grudgingly accepting that Abna was her superior in mathematics, she went on, "You work out the necessary coordinates and I'll feed them into the computer."

To Mexone seated at the controls, she called, "What's our present velocity?"

"Nearly 75 percent light speed," he answered.

"Good. By the time we reach light velocity I'll have our course fed in. Then we'll slip into the fourth dimension."

* * * *

Once again, on this strange journey across the galaxy, the Cosmic Crusaders and Curtar slept while the Ultra sped across thousands of light years as measured in normal space. The electronic brains linked to the computer carried it without any error on its way. The air conditioning worked perfectly.

For the sleepers on their couches, time had no meaning. It slipped by unnoticed, marked off only by the chronometer on the wall of the cabin.

It was not until they had all awake and were standing in front of the huge observation window that they noticed the large number of stars that were visible. In their earlier adventure they had come across an artificial configuration of seven suns all close together. But this was on a far larger scale. There appeared to be hundreds of them, of all colors and sizes, within a radius of two or three hundred light years.

"What is this?" Thania inquired, rubbing her eyes in sheer wonder.

"We seem to be in the middle of a large stellar cluster," Abna told her. "There are quite a number of these scattered across the galaxy, some even larger than this seems to be."

In a somewhat despondent tone, Curtar said, "Then in your language this is going to be like looking for a needle in a haystack."

"I'm afraid you may be right." While she spoke, the Amazon took a quick glance all around the view in front of them. "At least, I don't see any sign of the Kezbekían spaceship—or spaceships—in the vicinity at the moment."

"Let's hope that the earlier inscription the Derevanians made on this plate is more accurate than their later ones," Viona remarked. Picking up the magnifying glass she went over the mass of tiny dots again, her lips pressed into a tight line, her sapphire eyes taking in every little detail.

By magnifying the image to its maximum extent, she said. "According to this chart the double star we're looking for forms a triangle with two smaller stars."

"I'm afraid that doesn't help us much, Viona," the Amazon said, slipping an arm around Viona's shoulders. "This chart is a two-dimensional representation. What we see through the window is three-dimensional."

As Abna slowly decreased their tremendous velocity, keeping the deceleration within tolerable limits, they surveyed the entire scene, searching intently for any double star that might be visible.

It seemed a hopeless task. Finally, the Amazon asked, "Has anyone got any ideas how we can shorten this search?"

There was silence for a few minutes. Then Mexone said, "Since it's a double-star system we're looking for, is it possible to use the telescope and computer together?"

"In what way?" Abna inquired.

"It shouldn't be too difficult to set the telescope to make a complete scan of all the stars around the Ultra within say a hundred and fifty light-year radius and feed everything into the computer. If we program that to pick out every double-star system and give the result on a chart, it'll narrow down our search quite a bit."

"Of course it's possible," the Amazon exclaimed. "I designed both the telescope and computer systems. I know everything they're capable of. I'll do it right away."

Moving quickly to a bank of controls, she ran her yellow fingers swiftly over the keys, her face set in a mask of concentration. Stepping back, she said, "We'll have the chart in a couple of minutes."

Once the large sheet of paper slid out of the machine, she carried it over to the table and spread it out in front of them. Her violet eyes took in the situation at a single glance.

Finally she said, "Well, I suppose it could be worse. There are eleven double stars within a radius of a hundred and fifty light years. Since we've been able to improve our mathematics appreciably from that inscribed plate, I'd say it must be one of them."

She threw a swift glance in Abna's direction.

He nodded in complete agreement. "Furthermore," he added, "From what little we know of this race they clearly weren't searching for just any old planet on which to set down their colony. I think we should examine each of these systems in turn and look for something out of the ordinary."

"That might narrow it down a bit," the Amazon agreed.

Accordingly, each of the Crusaders took turns at the telescope using the highest magnification possible with the superb instrument. It was a slow and painstaking procedure and all the time the Amazon fretted with impatience.

Then Viona emitted a whoop of excitement. "This one seems strange."

The Amazon swung round sharply. "In what way, Viona?"

"There's a large red sun and a much smaller blue-white one. I know we've come across system like this before, but these stars are fairly widely separated and there seems to be only one planet."

"She's right as usual," Abna said. "All other double stars we've come across have had multiple planetary families, some orbiting one and the rest circling the companion sun."

Taking Viona's place, the Amazon carefully checked the coordinates and then crossed to the chart that the computer had produced. Her brow furrowed in thought, she examined it closely; then placed her finger on it.

"This is the system. Don't ask me why but I feel sure of it. It's not too far away from our present position—about twenty light years. I think we should head for it right away."

Everyone agreed. As they settled onto their couches, the Amazon said, "I must say this is one of the oddest journeys we've ever undertaken in the Ultra—tracing a single race all the way across the galaxy."

Nodding, Abna murmured, "I only hope it's worth it at the end."

There was no further conversation as they relaxed, falling asleep under the influence of the mild sedative drug administered by the hypodermic needles at the sides of the couches. This time the journey through the fourth dimension was comparatively short compared with their earlier trips.

All woke at almost the same time and this time it was Viona who slid adroitly from her couch and flicked the switch to bring back Earth-normal gravity. Crowding into the observation room they gazed out at the stellar system now directly ahead of them and approaching rapidly. The orange-red giant sun burned against the eternal dark to their left. On their right blazed the small white companion, its glare so vicious that it hurt their eyes to look directly at it.

CHAPTER VII

VIONA stared intently for a couple of minutes and then said wonderingly, "That's really strange. When I first observed that solitary planet through the telescope it was just coming into sight around the white star but now it's beginning to orbit around the other one."

The Amazon pursed her lips. "As I remember it, you're absolutely right, Viona. That means this world must be moving in a figure-of-eight orbit around both suns. Quite clearly, we have another peculiar world here."

"And that would indicate that this is the system marked on that metal plate," Thania interrupted.

Abna had remained silent throughout the conversation. Now, rubbing a hand down his cheek, he said, "Doesn't it also indicate something else to you?"

Puzzled, Viona asked, "What else, father?"

Straightening, Abna replied, "Here we find a planet performing a most peculiar orbit—circling two suns like a figure of eight. According to all the theories of planetary formation, such a thing is impossible. There is only one way this can happen."

"This is another world that doesn't belong here!" Viona cried in sudden realization.

"At some time in the past it must have been wandering free through space and been captured by these suns."

"Exactly," her father nodded. "There's a pattern beginning to form behind all of this. At the moment I can't think what the full implications are but I will in time."

"I agree this is one of the most intriguing situations I've ever encountered." The Amazon admitted. "If only it were possible to think like the ancient Derevanians and see the reasoning behind all of this."

"Perhaps, if we do succeed in reaching Derevan, we may learn the answer to that," Thania said.

Always anxious to be doing something, Viona said, "Then we investigate this world to see if the Derevanians ever did come here. Somehow, I'm positive they did. Even if this race was as advanced as they seem to be and probably won't have any need of our scientific help it will, at least, increase our store of knowledge."

There were no dissenters. They had come thus far, and no one had any intention of backing out now. Even the Amazon was fired with curiosity.

Taking over the controls, she guided the Ultra towards the lone planet. From a distance of a hundred thousand miles, it already showed a mottled surface—patches of green and brown with much larger blue areas that were clearly oceans. White clouds occasionally obscured their view of the surface.

"It looks very like Earth," The Amazon said. She ran her gaze over the figures on the left-hand side of the screen. "About 50 percent larger, two ice caps at the poles, atmosphere almost identical with Earth."

"Then the only factor which might worry us is the temperature," Abna cautioned.

"Since it's revolving in such a weird orbit that's bound to be extremely erratic."

"What makes you say that?" Thania asked. .

Smiling, Abna explained. "When it's going around that small hot star, the overall temperature will be much higher than we're used to and there will almost certainly be a lot of ultraviolet rays coming through the atmosphere. As it approaches the larger cooler star the surface temperature will then begin to drop quickly and once it passes behind that giant sun it may approach freezing point or below because then it will receive no radiation from that small sun."

"It doesn't sound like a very pleasant world," Thania replied. "I wonder why the Derevanians chose it to colonize?"

"We may find the answer to that question once we land," the Amazon told her. "Until then we can only surmise that there is something else about this world which was important to them. One odd thing I have noticed about it. It's moving much faster in its orbit than most other planets we've seen. I'd estimate it makes one complete revolution about both suns in less than two Earth months— about 40 days!"

In silence, they stood inspecting the mystery world as it rotated slowly before them.

As they drew closer its extremely rapid orbital motion became readily apparent to them all. It seemed to be fairly whizzing along.

Matching their velocity with it, the Amazon lowered the Ultra into the extensive atmosphere. Already details were becoming apparent.

Resting her weight on her arms, Viona called, "I'm sure I can see what look like cities down there. You think they may be a lot more advanced than that race we found in the veil nebula?"

Maintaining her concentration on the instruments, the Amazon replied, "I certainly hope so. I'd like to get some information from them, not only about their home planet but also this next planet marked on the chart, the first they apparently landed on when they set out on their voyage. I also haven't forgotten about the Kezbekians. They're almost certainly somewhere in this region and it may not be long before they find us."

With the air whining shrilly past the impervious hull, the Ultra skimmed over the tops of tall buildings and came gently to rest in an open space about a mile from the outskirts of the huge city.

Viona already had her weapons belt around her slim waist and stood waiting impatiently as the others donned theirs. Finally, they were ready. The airlock sprang open as Abna pushed the lever. One after the other, they descended the ladder into the orange light. Behind them, only a small crescent of the white companion sun was visible above the horizon. Even as they watched it dropped swiftly out of sight as the massive disc of the giant sun lifted into the heavens.

The breeze that swirled about them was hot and moist; a legacy of the period the world had spent revolving around the blue-white sun.

Breathing heavily, the Amazon wiped a hand across her brow. "Thankfully, the temperature should be going down soon now this world is swinging away from that other sun."

Checking the small Geiger counter, Abna said, "There's no indication of any radioactivity. A few stray cosmic rays but that's all." He took another instrument from his belt and thumbed a switch. "There is something else though."

"What's that?" Mexone asked. "Something dangerous?"

"I'm not sure. It's some form of radiation and it seems to be coming from that red sun. I've not come across anything like this before—a very low frequency emission."

The Amazon shrugged. "Whatever it is, I doubt if it can cause us any harm. Only the very high frequency radiation such as X-rays and gamma rays can cause any permanent damage if we're subjected to them for too long."

"Then if there's nothing to worry about," Viona interjected, "I suggest we take a look around in that city—see if there are any intelligent beings around."

While they were all naturally curious about this new world, Curtar seemed to be the most interested. His life's work had been dedicated to this search for the first intelligent life in the galaxy. Now, here he was—standing on one of the planets this race has visited—one that, out of the three they had found, seemed most likely to contain life of a high cultural and scientific level.

His old eyes took in everything as they made their way slowly towards the magnificent building in the near distance. Quickening his stride, he moved ahead of the others.

Keeping her voice down, Viona whispered, "Have you noticed something strange about that old man?"

When the others shook their heads, she went on, "Look at him. He seems to be gaining a new strength. He's walking faster and straighter than before."

After a quick scrutiny, the Amazon said, "You're right. Probably it's nothing more than the fact that he's now seeing the fulfillment of his life-long dream."

Compared with the last two planets they had visited, this one seemed a virtual paradise. Tall, graceful buildings stood on all sides, their architectural elegance far surpassing anything they had seen before.

The roadways shone as if made from glass, throwing the orange-red glow of the sun into their eyes as they stood at the end of a wide thoroughfare. Ornately decorated bridges spanned it at intervals beginning and ending halfway up the tall structures on either side. All around them, the air was filled with a low humming sound so faint they had to concentrate to hear it.

"It's certainly a beautiful place," Curtar said in a voice that seemed strangely stronger than before. "Truly a world befitting the Derevanians."

"Yet there seems to be no visible sign of them," Abna remarked, glancing around him. "I would have thought that everyone within miles would have heard and seen our arrival."

"I hope this isn't another world like Zerzura in that multiple sun system," Thania said. "That seemed to be a paradise yet there was no one there and there was also that sickness."

They approached one of the tallest buildings and stood looking at the wide decorated doors. The next moment there was a strange shimmering in the air and a tall figure materialized in front of them. It was impossible for them to mistake the grotesque winged form. It was undoubtedly a Derevanian who faced them. The unblinking eyes watched them with an expression of naked curiosity.

Moments later, an emotionless voice sounded in their heads. *Strangers—How came you here—to this of all worlds?*

The Amazon spoke up. "We found the lone world in the Cygnus Rift that we believe marked the end of your race's long journeying across the galaxy. There we found a star chart locating four suns and then your home world of Derevan."

And you have followed this route back to here?

"We have," Abna said shortly. "And we believe there are others who are also seeking Derevan. It may be they are not far from here at this moment."

The Derevanian seemed unperturbed by this news. *And what is it you seek here—or on Derevan—untold wealth or supreme power to rule over many worlds?*

Before the Amazon could speak, Curtar said quickly, "None of those things. I seek only knowledge, as do these others here with me."

Knowledge? That is something that comes in many forms. Some knowledge is gained over many millennia of observation—other knowledge may be given in a single instant of time. Know you that I am the last of my race on this world. All of the others have gone into that oblivion which awaits everyone, even those like us who are virtually immortal. There was knowledge here once. We brought with us many of the secrets of the universe.

"Then where is this information now?" the Amazon asked.

Without answering, the Derevanian turned slightly. One claw-like hand lifted and pointed into the distance. Peering through the red light, they made out the large building near the far end of the wide avenue. Rather it had once been a building. Now it was merely a blackened ruin, a single ugly blot on the otherwise beautiful landscape.

That is where all our writings were held but then it was decided that such information could prove catastrophic if it should ever fall into the wrong hands. We destroyed it so that it could never be used for death and destruction. Too many races have, since us, appeared in the galaxy their minds and thoughts intent only on killing and the enslavement of others. We could not allow that. Accordingly it was decided that before all of us here died out, it should be destroyed.

Over the billions of years that have passed since we came here, others have come seeking our knowledge. When we refused to give it to them, they destroyed us with their weapons of destruction so that now, I am now the only one left of our once-proud race.

Despite their intense disappointment at this answer both the Amazon and Abna could understand the wisdom and logic behind it.

After a few moments, the mental voice continued, *All of you are welcome to remain here as long as you wish but I would warn against the delirium which comes at the intersection. If you should decide to remain—be warned.*

The Amazon opened her mouth to ask more; then closed it tightly. She would be speaking to no one. The figure had vanished as quickly, and mysteriously, as it had appeared.

"What under the stars do you think he meant by that last remark?" Thania asked.

The Amazon shrugged her slim shoulders. "Either there is something important here which he doesn't want us to find and he was trying to get rid of us—or there's something odd about this planet which has aroused my scientific curiosity."

"Don't you think we should head for that next sun? If the star chart is correct that would be the first these people landed on after setting out." Curtar commented. "If that creature spoke the truth, there's obviously no point in searching any further. It would simply be a waste of time." There was a note of impatience in his tone.

He seemed more filled with purpose than the Crusaders had noticed before—as if he had really gained a new lease of strength and vitality.

The Amazon shook her blonde head. "We've only just arrived here, Curtar. At the moment, I don't know whether to believe that Derevanian or not when he claimed all of the records here were destroyed in that fire."

"But we've no reason to think he was lying," Abna put in. "I agree with Curtar. Why waste time? It's clear there's nothing here to help us refine our coordinates of that next sun on the list."

"Perhaps not. But don't you want to know what he was talking about when he mentioned some delirium at the point of intersection? To my mind there's something baffling about this planet and I intend to wait and see what it is."

"Very well," Abna agreed reluctantly. The Amazon was in one of her determined moods and when she was like this nothing would sway her from her purpose.

"So what is this intersection he spoke about where this so-called madness is supposed to occur?" Viona asked.

"Isn't it obvious what he meant? There's only one intersection I know of in this entire system. We've seen it for ourselves—where the two orbits intersect in their figure-of-eight configuration."

"You think that something really drastic happens whenever that occurs, Amazon?" Thania asked, a trace of growing excitement in her voice.

"I'm sure of it. As to its nature, that's something I intend to find out for myself."

Glancing at the city around him, Abna said, "Then according to the time we calculated for this planet to orbit both suns—a little less than two Earth months—and allowing for the fact that it was already well into its orbit towards this red giant when we landed, I'd say we'll have to wait about ten or eleven days before we reach that point."

"So what do you propose we should do in the interim?" Viona inquired. The prospect of simply sitting around doing nothing irked her.

"Study this world," her mother replied decisively. "If we ever do locate Derevan, I'd like to know a little more about this race before we get there and this would seem as good a chance as any."

The days that followed were unlike any they had ever spent before. It was not long before the vagaries of this strange world made themselves known. The days and nights were roughly the same length as those on Earth. The blue-white sun made briefer and briefer appearances above the horizon as they passed behind the much larger red sun. The overall temperature continued to fall until by the time the companion sun disappeared altogether from their view, the days were almost invariably foggy and cool.

The nights, however, were frosty and clear. The dense fog swiftly froze out of the atmosphere forming a glistening white layer over everything and the stars were brilliant in the crystal-clear heavens.

The cities they examined were all beautifully laid out yet there were wide differences among them. Here they came across one that closely resembled old Baghdad with lofty spires and minarets. Elsewhere they flew over one similar to modern New York with rearing skyscrapers. In addition to these there were also numerous much smaller villages set in rolling countryside. Altogether it seemed an idyllic world, yet as the days passed, both the Amazon and Abna experienced a growing tension.

All of what they saw indicated that in days gone by, the Derevanians had enjoyed both a rural and an urban existence. One fact that puzzled them at first was that all of the windows were far larger than similar buildings on Earth. .

When Thania drew their attention to this it was Viona who supplied the answer.

"We're forgetting that these people were a winged race. Doubtless they flew in and out of the windows just as we use doors."

They saw no sign of that solitary survivor of this once-great race that had built these fantastic cities and turned the planet into a Garden of Eden. At times, they thought they had simply imagined him.

Then the morning came when the tip of the white sun showed above the horizon.

Viona was the first to see it through the observation window just after they had finished their meal. The Amazon and Abna came over to stand beside her.

"A truly strange system," Abna observed. "Another few days and the temperature out there will be unbearable for us unless we use refrigeration units in our suits."

"Somehow I think we've seen most of what this world has to offer," the Amazon commented. "What strikes me as odd is the fact that overall it's little different from dozens of other worlds we've seen. Why would the Derevanians choose this particular one out of hundreds of others? The only link among the three we've already visited is that at one time they were all lone planets wandering the galaxy without a parent sun."

"There has to be something significant about that," Abna nodded. "But for the life of me I can't see what it is."

Thereafter, as the days passed, the tiny white sun rose higher and higher into the heavens. Once the temperature inside the vessel rose above the 25-degree mark, the refrigeration units kicked in. Outside, the glare from the white sun became intolerable. It was impossible to look at it without wearing dark goggles.

Seated in the observation well of the Ultra, the Amazon remarked, "Another eight hours and we should pass through the intersection point of this orbit. I think we should all be prepared for it."

"You believe that Derevanian when he warned us against it?" Thania asked.

"Somehow, I think you're right, Vi." Abna stood beside the data-gathering instruments, all of which were focused on the white sun. There was an expression of deep concern on his handsome features. "You recall we detected an odd radiation coming from that red sun yonder."

The Amazon nodded. "I remember. It was a very low-frequency radiation."

"Well, I've just checked this other sun. It's emitting something very similar—and it's quite a powerful emission."

"Is it the same wavelength?" Mexone asked. He came over and looked for himself, finally shaking his head. "No, it's not—it's slightly different. But you're right about the power. That sun must be blasting it out at a terrific rate."

He put his hand out to point a finger at the figures—then jerked it back as though he had been stung, uttering a startled yell. His face was twisted into a mask of sheer horror. Staggering back, he rubbed his eyes.

"What's wrong, Mexone?" Viona was by his side in an instant, holding one arm tightly.

"For a moment I thought that—no, it must have been a trick of the light."

The Amazon regarded him with a serious expression on her face. "It was something more than that, Mexone. Out with it. What happened?"

For a moment, Mexone seemed determined not to answer her question. Then, somewhat sheepishly, he muttered, "It was as if some fierce animal was there right in front of me. It made a lunge at me. But that's impossible. It must have been—"

The next second, Thania uttered a frightful scream. She was staring, wide-eyed, at the cabin wall, desperately trying to reach for her utility belt hanging a few feet away, her fingers scrabbling for the weapon.

Before the Amazon could register what was happening, a white-faced Viona, her lips twisting into a grimace of horrified disbelief, had lunged at Abna, her hands clamping tightly about his throat. For a horror-stricken instant the Amazon stood rooted to the spot, unable to move.

There was a curious ringing inside her head and the next moment everything changed. The Crusaders were no longer there. Instead, she saw a hideously disfigured creature struggling with a much larger monster. Equally ugly forms were standing in menacing attitudes around her and other snake-like things were crawling out of the solid walls.

Of all the Crusaders, only Abna's supreme mental capabilities saved him at that moment. His mind instantly recognized what was happening. This was not real. Everything he saw was a hallucination. Within a split second his mind had put up a defense against this insidious force that had attacked them.

Swiftly, he summoned all of his mental efforts into a state of intense concentration. Everything wavered and then returned to normal, but it was clear that all of the others had fallen beneath this intense hallucinatory effect and were unable to resist it. Reaching up, he tore his daughter's hands from around his throat, struggling to ignore the expression of utter horror on her face. Dragging her with him, he took down a length of the nylon rope they used for climbing obstacles. Pinning her arms behind her back, he swiftly tied her wrists and legs laying her on her stomach on the floor and then turned his attention to the others.

Curtar, his mouth hanging slackly open, eyes staring, was easily subdued as were Thania and Mexone. The Amazon, however, was a different matter. Her strength was virtually the equal of his and her hallucinatory state gave her even more.

As she came at him, her hands outstretched, fingers curved into claws, he knew she was not seeing him but some monstrous thing intent on attacking her. He was also at a disadvantage since he had no wish to harm her. In the thrall of this intense hallucinatory force she had no idea what she was doing. He had no inkling what she was seeing at that moment but there was an intense loathing mirrored in her violet eyes.

As she reached him, he grabbed her arms intending to pin her to the floor and hope to hold her there. But she twisted at the last moment, bending forward and ducking under him. With an almost effortless movement she straightened, lifting him off his feet and throwing him over her back, sending him crashing against the instrument console.

Before he could get to his feet she had darted to her right, seizing a long steel bar. Grasping one end she easily bent the bar into the shape of a hook, the muscles of her arms flexing beneath the skin-tight outfit she wore. Snarling viciously, gripping the hook in both hands, she came towards him again.

Drawing back her arms, she swung the steel bar at his head, trying to hook it around his neck. Savagely, he caught it and somehow managed to thrust himself upright. Gritting his teeth, he said insistently, "This is me, Vi—Abna, your husband. All of this is simply an illusion, a hallucination. Use your mind and will to fight it!"

Her lips were drawn back across her bared teeth like some animal as she forced him back. Temporarily, completely dominated by this hallucinatory effect, her strength was even greater than his.

Desperately, he tried to figure out what to do. In her present state she could easily overcome him and cause injury to the others and damage to the ship. Apart for knocking her out, he could think of nothing.

He tried one final risky attempt. Releasing his hold on the bar, he clamped his hands tightly on each side of her head. Using his tremendous mental abilities, he meshed his mind directly with hers.

"Resist it, Vi. You can do it. None of this is real. All you have to do is recognize that, focus all of your will on it."

For a moment, he thought he had failed. Her violet eyes still glared savagely into his. Then, incredibly, a spark of sanity returned. Transferring his hands to her shoulders, he shook her. Her lips moved but for a moment no words came out.

Then: "Abna? Is that you? But…what's happening? I thought you were some horrible monster that, somehow, we had been attacked by aliens. And the others were the same."

"I know. I was almost caught in it. This is some kind of intense hallucination. I think I know the cause but first things first. I need you to help me get the Ultra into space."

For an instant, he thought the Amazon was slipping back into the illusion but then she firmed her jaw, and nodded.

A moment later, the Amazon fed a copper cube into the energy matrix as Abna flicked down a switch, transferring the energy to the engines. Smoothly, the Ultra lifted from the surface, rising into the atmosphere. Slipping on his goggles as the glaring white disc of the sun glared directly into his eyes, he guided the huge spaceship towards outer space. Swiftly, the disc of the planet dwindled behind them.

Deftly he turned the nose of the Ultra away from the orbit of the planet. Throwing a swift glance over his shoulder, he saw that the others were slowly coming back to normal. The frenzied expressions on their faces were being replaced by looks of mystified wonder.

As the Amazon started to slip into the seat beside him, he said, "I think you can untie the others, Vi. We're out of that hallucinatory effect now. I don't think it will have any lasting effects."

Once this was done, Viona asked, "Something happened to us back there. Everyone I saw was... something monstrous. What was it?"

"It was what that Derevanian warned us against—what your mother was so anxious to discover. Those ultra low-frequency waves being emitted from the two suns—I suppose I should have realized their significance before and warned you against it, Vi."

"What exactly do you mean?" the Amazon queried, a little angered at his implied suggestion that all of this had been the fault of her innate scientific curiosity.

"Those low-frequency waves are in the same region of the electromagnetic spectrum as the alpha and theta waves emitted by the human brain."

A short silence followed as the others digested this statement. Then Viona said, "And at the intersection point that is where they're strongest and somehow they combine with each other affecting our minds."

"Making us see things that weren't really there," Mexone added.

Abna nodded. "Thankfully my will was strong enough to throw them off but there's no doubt the rest of you may have killed—or seriously injured—each other if I hadn't tied you up."

"Then I suggest we now leave this system and head for the next sun," the Amazon butted in. "I had hoped there might have been a further chart somewhere in one of those cities. If there ever had been one, however, my guess is that it was destroyed by fire with every other bit of information. Now we—" She broke off abruptly as Thania gave a sudden urgent shout.

"Spaceships! Two of them coming towards us from the direction of the white sun!"

CHAPTER VIII

SHIFTING his gaze, Abna spotted them instantly. There was no mistaking the ugly, squat shapes. They were undoubtedly Kezbekian vessels, and it was clear from their trajectory that the Ultra had been seen.

"Let's go and get them," the Amazon muttered harshly, a touch of iron determination in her tone. "Make sure the repeller shield is up at maximum power and everyone at their posts. Now we can—"

"No!" Abna interrupted sharply. "There's no need to fight them and we have to remember those stasis bombs they possess. We can't fight them if we get caught in one of those again."

"You're not suggesting we should turn and run with our tails between our legs?" the Amazon said angrily.

"I'm suggesting there's a better and surer way of destroying them." Even as he spoke, Abna was turning the Ultra away from the rapidly approaching spaceships.

"I don't know what you're thinking of doing but this is the first time I've ever run from an enemy." Her face set in angry lines, the Amazon stood silently as Abna headed the Ultra towards the orbit of the strange planet. Deliberately, he slowed the massive spacecraft allowing the enemy vessels to gain on him.

"They're almost within firing range of us!" Viona called.

Tensely, the Amazon said, "I only hope you know what you're doing."

Nodding, Abna replied, "Just hang on." To Mexone, he called: "Are those vessels still on our tail?"

"Yes. They're still there and gaining on us. They're definitely putting on speed."

"Good. Now we'll lead them into the intersection. It's completely invisible so they won't know what's hit them before it's too late."

"You think it will work?" Thania asked, a trifle dubiously, glancing at Abna.

"I'm sure it will. It had a dramatic illusory effect on us and I'm confident we possess far more brilliant minds than they do. If it could affect us to that degree, it will have ten times greater effect on them."

Such were Abna's supreme mathematical skills that, even though there was nothing visible to indicate where it was, he had the exact position of the intersection in his sights.

"Stand by for acceleration," he ordered a few moments later. Swiftly, the Crusaders grasped any immovable object within reach with the Amazon holding tightly to Curtar.

With a mighty roar, the Ultra suddenly jumped forward, swinging in a tight curve. Behind it, the two enemy vessels swept forward straight into the region of powerful hallucinatory radiation from the two suns.

Through the wide viewing window, the Cosmic Crusaders saw the two spaceships abruptly spin out of control. What horrific images the crews of those vessels were seeing, they had no idea. But clearly it was sufficient for them to lose all control.

Already the two ships were spiraling towards the giant red sun, accelerating all the time as its intense gravitational field caught them in its irresistible grip.

Getting out of his chair, Abna joined the others. The Kezbekian spacecraft were now little more than black dots silhouetted against the glare of the orange-red disc. The Amazon watched them with a grim smile on her lips. Finally, she said grudgingly, "I'll admit that was another excellent idea of yours, Abna. Somehow, I think that even when they recover from those hallucinations, they won't be able to pull away from that sun."

"That's certainly how it looks from here." Thania spoke from the far end of the controls, her eyes taking in every little detail. Then she went on, "So now we've finished off those Kezbekians, do we head for this other world—the one where the Deravanians first made planetfall on their outward journey?"

"I think we should first have a meal," the Amazon suggested. "It's some time since we've eaten and with the destruction of those ships there's now no need to hurry."

While they sat around the table, they discussed the situation in which they found themselves. Firstly, the Amazon said, "I'm naturally disappointed that we found no records on that planet. If there had been any, like on those other two worlds, we might have been able to refine our trajectory towards this other sun even further. As it is, we must rely entirely on the chart given on that metal plate which is almost certainly billions of years out of date."

"And it means we have another long journey ahead of us through hyperspace," Thania interjected between mouthfuls.

At the end of the table, Curtar glanced up, a worried expression on his face. "I trust this doesn't mean you're thinking of giving up this search?"

"Not on your life," Abna affirmed emphatically. "Now we've come this far, we go on to the very end." He regarded the Kezbekian studiously for a few moments. "You evidently know more of this race than we do, Curtar. What exactly do you expect to find if we reach Derevan?"

The old man shrugged. "I'm not sure. Perhaps I'd hoped that we might find colonies of these people along the way but apart from that solitary survivor we've found nothing. One settlement destroyed by a cosmic storm and another that has degenerated back to the savage state. It may be we'll find the same on this other world and also on Derevan."

"Let's not become too despondent," the Amazon put in. "There are still several loose ends to tie up before we have the full picture, questions to which we have no answers. Why did they decide, at some stage of their history, to send out these large groups? Why did they choose this particular route through the galaxy? What's the reason behind this strange coincidence that all of the planets we've so far discovered have at one time been wandering free through space with no attendant sun?"

She looked to Abna and Viona for possible answers but it was Thania who spoke first.

"Could it be that the Derevanians were aware of those races which inhabited these worlds, that they were people like themselves who chose to go out to the stars rather than destroying themselves in a nuclear holocaust?"

Pushing his empty plate away, Abna said, "That's quite logical, Thania. However, another reason might be that only on certain worlds are conditions right for them to retain their immortality. At the moment, we don't know how they achieved it. Perhaps it's in their genes—or it may be that each of these planets emits some form of unknown radiation which accounts for it."

"Or as in our own case," the Amazon put in, "we extended our lifespan considerably by biogenetic methods. Right now, we're faced with so many unknowns it's impossible to reach the correct solution. I think that before we retire, we should examine that plate more closely, get as accurate a fix as we can on that next sun allowing for any change in position during the interim and then head for it."

Her suggestion was immediately put into action. The necessary co-ordinates were worked out and fed into the computer and, as before, they settled themselves on the couches, ready for the transition into the fourth dimension.

* * * *

Somewhere on the outer fringes of the galaxy there was a sudden convulsion of space, a vague shimmer of luminosity as a huge silver shape materialized abruptly out of apparent nothingness. It was the Ultra, its interior lights still burning. With no nearby sun to reflect light from its immaculate surface it scarcely showed against the utter blackness of space.

The vessel had covered almost a thousand light years, traveling at many times the speed of light. Now its velocity was 98 percent light-velocity and a few seconds later, operated by the perfect electronic brains on board, the forward rockets fired. Gradually, they slowed the spaceship's tremendous forward momentum.

Here, on the outer galactic rim the stars were few and far between. Beyond those that were visible to the Crusaders, once they had stirred and taken their normal places, lay the Great Dark that stretched for more than two million light years to the nearest great galaxy—the spiral nebula in Andromeda.

Staring out through the window, Viona remarked, "You know this reminds me of that time we spent close to that seetee sun. It was also on the edge of our galaxy and the view we had then of the Andromeda Spiral is very similar to this."

"I agree," The Amazon replied musingly. "But there are very few seetee suns in the galaxy. That one was probably an interloper from the gulf out there."

"Meaning that it's unlikely we'll find one here," Viona said. "I mean if we did it would certainly mark it out from any others, just like those two other stars we've visited."

"Why should there be very few of these stars in the galaxy?" Thania inquired eagerly, always thirsting for knowledge. Being the youngest and most recent of the Cosmic Crusaders she knew that there were several things about which she knew and understood little.

"It's because the atoms which make up seetee matter are the opposite of normal matter," Abna explained. "We're made up of atoms containing protons and neutrons in the positively charged nucleus with negative electrons orbiting it. With contraterrene matter, the nucleus consists of anti-protons and anti-neutrons and is negatively charged and instead of electrons there are positrons that have a positive electrical charge. If a seetee sun and a normal sun were to collide, they would literally destroy each other in a tremendous blaze of radiation."

"It's possible there might be entire galaxies composed of contraterrene matter," interjected the Amazon, "since they would be separated from any others by millions of light years of empty space. Indeed, a number of truly massive explosions have been observed which could, in theory, be due to the collision between a seetee and a normal galaxy. Anyway, that's enough of theoretical cosmology for the moment. Let's take a look around and see what we have here."

There was not much for them to see. A handful of suns were visible, standing out against the intergalactic gulf beyond. None appeared to be other than ordinary stars.

The Amazon experienced a sense of disappointment. Either the stellar system they were searching for had been carried much further away by the galactic rotation—or there was something amiss with their calculations.

"There doesn't appear to be anything in this vicinity which is out of the ordinary," she muttered finally.

After a few moments perusal, Mexone said, "What about that star over there to the right?"

The Amazon stared in the direction of his pointing finger. "To be honest, I don't see anything strange about it," she said, shaking her blonde head. "Whatever it is, it's very faint. I'd say there's very little visible radiation being emitted by it. By far most of it is coming through in the far infrared. It's almost certainly a small old sun nearing the end of its evolutionary life."

"That's just what I would have thought," Mexone conceded. "But I've examined it with the ultra-mass detector. Unless there's some fault with the instrument—which doesn't seem likely—it has a mass of more than sixty times that of your sun."

"That's utterly impossible," the Amazon declared. "You must have made a mistake with the readings." She leaned forward slightly, examining the instrument carefully. When she straightened there was a look of mystification on her beautiful features.

"There seems to be no mistake," she said, signaling to Abna to check for himself.

Nodding, he made a wry face. "All I can suggest is that it's either a massive star just forming out of a protostellar gas-and-dust cloud, or it's the most peculiar object I've ever seen. It's definitely worth a closer look. How far away is it?"

"Not far," Mexone replied. "About seven light years."

"That's only a short jump through hyperspace. I think I'll sit this one out. I seem to have been asleep traveling through the fourth dimension for almost half of this journey."

Since the rest of them, with the exception of Curtar, felt the same, they merely relaxed on their couches as they accelerated to light speed and then entered the weird grey nothingness that was hyperspace. It was not a pleasant experience but both the Amazon and Abna had done it before. Although they were traveling at many times the speed of light, time had no meaning—and to them it seemed they were simply standing still, suspended utterly motionless in this eerie continuum.

Their emergence into normal space-time was virtually instantaneous. One moment they were in hyperspace and a split second later the entire cabin was flooded with a pale red light. Now the curious object was a huge disc almost directly ahead of them.

"We're almost on top of it," Abna yelled. "I'll have to give the Ultra maximum deceleration. Better be prepared for this—it isn't going to be pleasant."

Swiftly, he ran his fingers over the controls giving maximum power to the retarding rockets. The Ultra shuddered throughout its entire length. To the passengers it seemed the restraining straps would snap as their bodies were thrust forward. It was as if a massive weight sat on their backs, crushing them in their couches.

Gasping with the tremendous strain, they struggled to breathe. With a tremendous effort, the Amazon managed to turn her head. Curtar was unconscious. The others were fighting the strain with every ounce of strength in their superhuman bodies.

Slowly, the strain diminished. The needle on the circular dial just above the Amazon's head seemed blurred. Savagely, she forced her vision to right itself. With a sigh of relief, she saw they were now traveling at less than five thousand miles a minute.

By the time they entered the control room the nearby sun was so large that even though they were more than a 100 million miles from the surface, it filled the entire viewing screen.

Huge sunspots, large enough to swallow Earth's Sun dotted its pale surface while vast whirlpools of hotter gas spun and twisted within the chromosphere, spearing high into the corona.

In an awed voice, Viona said, "That sun must have a diameter of more than three hundred million miles."

"That's a fairly accurate figure," said the Amazon. "If it were in my solar system, both Earth and Mars would be inside it."

"Then if this is the star we're looking for there should be some sign of one or more planets." Thania remarked. "So far I haven't seen any."

"With a sun as large as that, it's possible two or three worlds might be occulted by it at the moment," Abna suggested. "But what puzzles me more is the extremely low surface temperature. New stars born out of large gas clouds emit mainly infrared radiation since their temperatures are so low. In addition, they're surrounded by dust usually in the form of graphite grains that shrouds the newly-formed star. Radiation from the star heats these and it's then emitted as long-wave infrared light."

"Then what is it that puzzles you?" Mexone asked.

"The fact that such stars as that are very small objects, with masses not much greater than Sol. Huge stars like this are much hotter and whiter."

"Right now, I'm more interested in any planets it may have," the Amazon snapped, "rather than discussing anomalies about its temperature. Has anyone spotted any yet?"

All replies were negative. Remaining at a constant distance from the supergiant sun, they circled it slowly, all eyes searching the entire region for any tiny pinprick of light.

There was nothing.

As far as they were able to determine, this sun was totally devoid of any planets. After an hour of examining the empty space surrounding the sun, Viona said disappointedly, "Then it would seem there are just two possibilities. Either this is not the sun marked on the Derevanian star chart—or when that race first came here, the sun wasn't as large as it is now. They could have settled here, unaware that the sun was about to expand and engulf their entire world."

"Viona—you're a genius," the Amazon declared. "Of course, that's the answer. Why didn't we think of it before? There is a planet here only we can't see it because it's revolving inside that tenuous solar atmosphere!"

Abna rubbed his chin in deep thought, turning that idea over in his mind. Finally, he nodded slowly. "It's quite possible, I suppose," he agreed. "We've come across such a bizarre situation before, and I'd say the temperature just inside the chromosphere may be low enough for a race to survive under such peculiar conditions."

"But if we can't see it, how do we find it?" Thanía interrupted.

The Amazon thought for a moment. "We could use the mass detector. It's certainly sufficiently sensitive to pick out the mass of a planet even if it is superimposed on the much larger mass of that sun."

As Abna brought the Ultra a little closer to the solar surface before putting the spacecraft into an orbit around it, the Amazon took her place in front of the mass detector, flicking down a switch and adjusting it to its highest degree of sensitivity.

Aiming it towards the equatorial region where it was most likely any planetary orbit would be, she waited, her gaze fixed on the thin red needle in the center of the dial.

Viona and Thania stood just behind her, waiting intently for the twitch of the needle that would indicate something of planetary size orbiting within the chromosphere.

Minutes passed and still the pointer remained stationary.

"Anything showing yet?" Mexone called.

"Nothing," the Amazon replied. "But considering it could be anywhere within a huge orbit, it isn't surprising. Even if we do pick it up, the deflection will be extremely small. It will be like looking for a speck of dust passing across my own sun."

After a quarter of an hour had passed without any discernable kick of the needle, the Amazon was beginning to have doubts. Having designed the detector, she knew its limitations. Rubbing her eyes, she sat back in her chair.

"There it is!" Thania yelled abruptly, excitement in her voice.

The Amazon gave a slight nod. The pointer had moved to the right from its central position. The deflection was only small but there was no mistaking it. Flicking her gaze towards the distance indicator, she made a rapid mental calculation.

"It's about three hundred miles inside that layer of gases," she said tightly. "Roughly the same size as Earth."

"Do you think it will be possible for us to land on it?" Viona sounded dubious.

It was Abna who answered her. "Considering the extremely low temperature, it should be possible. Whether we could exist outside the ship is more problematical, even with refrigerated spacesuits."

"But at least it's worth a try."

Abna grinned. "If the Derevanians are still here, of course it's worth a try."

Following the course of the concealed planet by means of the mass detector, the Ultra headed for the mighty red disc of the sun. A nearby sunspot lay close to where the planet was located, and it was towards this that Abna guided the spacecraft.

CHAPTER IX

LIKE a great silver fish, the Ultra dived into the gaping sunspot. As it did so, the Amazon kept a close watch on the outside temperature. On a number of previous occasions, she had been as close as this to a sun—but here there was a difference.

Outside, the temperature was barely 400 degrees. Hot—but by using the highly efficient cooling effect of their refrigerated suits, it might just be possible to tolerate it for very short periods. The only one she was really worried about was Curtar. Clearly, he would not be used to such extreme conditions.

Around them was the vicious glare of the tenuous gases, blotting out everything in the galaxy outside. Pulling on the dark goggles, she motioned to the others to do the same and it was not long before they spotted the dark shape of the planet almost directly in front of them. Dexterously, Abna maneuvered the Ultra towards it.

Even with the goggles it was not easy to make out many details. Through the portholes and visiscreen, the glaring red light flooded the cabin, giving their features a ghastly look. Eyes narrowed, they all watched as the strange world drifted closer.

There was no sign of any oceans or rivers, which was not surprising since any surface water would have long since boiled away.

"What do you make of it, Abna?" the Amazon asked. "Do you think any kind of intelligent life could possible live down there?"

"If we believe in the theory that life adapts itself to its external environment, then I suppose it may be possible. We know the Derevanians attained the highest possible level of scientific attainment. What puzzles me is why they should choose to inhabit such a hostile region in the galaxy—unless they became so reclusive they wanted to shut themselves away from all other races."

"Or as we suggested before, this sun suddenly swelled, engulfing them without warning, and there was nothing they could do about it," Thania conjectured.

"That could be it," conceded the Amazon. Squinting through the glare, she went on, pointing, "No wonder we can't make out any details on that planetary surface. The entire world is covered by some sort of dense material. I wonder what that can be?"

"Isn't it obvious?" Abna said. "That must be some form of heat-reflecting shell. Just as a mirror reflects any light that falls upon it that stuff throws back all of the heat, no doubt making the true surface of the planet inside quite bearable."

Pursing her lips, Viona asked, "Then if that covers the entire planet, how are we going to reach the surface?"

"A good question," replied her mother. "At the moment, I've no idea how we can penetrate it." By now the Ultra was only ten miles above the heat radiating shell. "From the look of it, there's no way we can do that, unless—"

There was a sudden violent jerk as the spaceship came to an abrupt halt, throwing them all forward against the instruments. The engines shrilled as they began to strain against the immovable hold. Eardrums vibrating agonizingly under the violence of that high-pitched whine, the Amazon yelled, "Cut the engines, Abna, unless you want to overload them. We're caught in some kind of tractor beam and it's far too strong for us to break out of it."

Swiftly, Abna pulled back the lever. Silence returned but their ears still registered that harsh scream long after it had faded. For a few moments they hung there—completely motionless. Then, slowly, the Ultra began to descend.

Shakily, Viona moved to one of the ports and glanced down. When they were less than a hundred feet above the surrounding shell, a huge section of it slid aside. Smoothly, the Ultra passed through it. All sight of the swirling chromospheric gases vanished as the square section slid shut above them. As light as a feather, the Ultra sank towards the true surface of the planet still some distance away.

Directly beneath them they saw a large clear area and ten minutes later, they landed with scarcely a bump.

"Well, at least we're safe and in one piece," Thania murmured. "I wonder what they intend to do with us now that we're here."

"I think we'll soon find out." Mexone inclined his head towards the scene outside. All around them were graceful buildings with Doric arches and colonnades of what looked like white marble. Pale yellow light suffused the whole scene although it was impossible for them to determine its origin.

A small group of figures was advancing towards the Ultra. Even from a distance, their outlines were familiar to the Crusaders. From behind them, Curtar said softly, "We were right. This is the first world they came to. Now we may learn something of Derevan."

"Always assuming they're friendly towards unexpected visitors to their world," Viona said grimly. "At the moment, they seem to have us trapped here."

The group stopped fifty yards away and one of the Derevanians signaled that they were to open the airlock and come outside to join them.

"They seem to be friendly," Abna observed. "Do you think it's necessary to meet them with weapons?"

"I trust no one," the Amazon retorted stiffly. So saying she took down her weapon belt and strapped it on.

Abna frowned. Yet although he did not share the Amazon's attitude towards the sanctity of human life, he finally decided that in this case it might be a good thing to take precautions. In the past the people they had encountered were humanoid but with an avian species it was impossible to really get into their minds.

At the airlock, they waited until both inner and outer doors slid open and the ladder had descended to the ground. Climbing down, one after the other, they were surprised to find that the temperature was quite normal.

For a moment, the Amazon surveyed the buildings on all sides. Had she not known she was on an alien planet some seventy thousand light years from Earth, she would have thought she was standing in the middle of ancient Athens or Rome. Long colonnades of marble pillars stretched away in all directions with wide streets and squares. There were no doors to any of the buildings, only the large open windows they had seen on the last planet they had visited, all testifying to the avian ancestry of the Derevanians.

Now they could see the creatures more clearly, the Amazon remarked, "Why they're old, much older even than the one on that last planet."

"Yet they were supposed to be immortal," Mexone butted in.

"But after several billion years I guess we should expect some changes," Abna commented. "I—" He stopped as a voice sounded inside their heads.

Where are you from, strangers? We note that you are a totally different species to us.

Before any of them could reply, a second voice continued: *We sensed your arrival some time ago. We do not welcome other races to our world. Some have come over the millennia and those we have been forced to destroy. We have allowed you to come since, although one of you carries a primitive weapon, you appear different to the others. Now that we have satisfied ourselves about you, you must leave.*

The Amazon and Abna both stepped forward and it was the Amazon who spoke first, her right hand close to the blaster at her waist. "All we seek is information. We've traveled thousands of light years across the galaxy searching for Derevan."

A gust of expression showed momentarily on the faces of the Derevanians but being a birdlike race, it was impossible to guess what it meant—surprise, fear, anger? The Amazon was unable to decide.

We know nothing of Derevan. All contact with our home world has been lost for countless ages. Whether it still exists we do not know. Long ago we tried to enter the final metamorphosis in our evolution but, too late, we discovered there are certain radiations emitted by this sun, which make it impossible.

Thus, we are as you see us now, continued another voice, *doomed to remain in this material form, shut away from the rest of the galaxy. Those who believe that immortality is a blessing are wrong. For us death, the end of all things, would be preferable to this existence. Now you must leave. We will tell you no more.*

Abna shrugged his broad shoulders and made to turn but the Amazon snapped sharply, "Are you just going to walk away? There are a lot of other questions, important questions, I want to ask."

"And how do you think you're going to get anything more out of them? Threaten them with protonic blasters, blow a few holes in these magnificent buildings? Somehow, I don't think that will work. You can't threaten people with extinction when, as they've just said, that is exactly what they want more than anything."

The Amazon bit back on an angry retort. Although she did not want to admit it, for once she was beaten. What her husband said was absolutely true. There was no point in trying to force these creatures to speak by means of a show of force. Releasing her tight-fisted hold on the weapon, she allowed it to fall back into its holster and then spun on her heel, her lovely features set into mask of resentment.

Returning to the Ultra, they climbed on board, drawing up the ladder and closing the airlock securely. Once inside the controls room, they waited. A few moments later, the huge ship began to lift. The aperture in the outer shell opened and they were inside the outermost layer of the sun once more. Pressing the button, Abna started the mighty engines, turning the vessel into a tight curve and out into empty space.

A trace of bitterness in her voice, the Amazon said, "Well that was a complete waste of time." Glancing over her shoulder, she added, "I'm sorry, Curtar. I really hoped we might learn a lot more from those Derevanians. Unfortunately, they proved to be the most inhospitable and uncommunicative race I've ever encountered."

"You did your best, Amazon," the Kezbekian replied. "We can only hope we get a better reception on Derevan—if we ever find it."

Sitting over the instruments, Abna commented, "We did learn something from them, Vi."

Still smarting with indignation, the Amazon asked, "And what might that be? To me they seemed to be so ancient they were rapidly becoming senile."

"That's as maybe. But I'm sure they still possess some tremendous power—and by that I mean weapons—if they should choose to use them."

"How do you make that out?" Viona inquired, mystified. "We saw nothing like that."

Abna smiled grimly. "Don't you remember how he referred to your mother's blaster as a primitive weapon? That's one of the most advanced and powerful hand weapons we possess."

Twisting her lips a little, the Amazon asked, "Anything else?"

"Yes. They said something that struck me as very odd—that some form of radiation from this sun prevented them from undergoing the final metamorphosis in their evolution. I've no idea what form this transubstantiation would take but it must be something pretty drastic.

I also reckon that it's because of this that they have this belligerent attitude. They're still immortal, they may even look upon themselves as gods, lords of creation—but something extremely important has been denied them."

The Amazon sniffed. "That may be so—but I don't like being dictated to in that off-hand way."

Abna laid a hand on her arm. "I can understand your feelings, Vi—but there was literally nothing else we could do. We're dealing with an entirely alien species. Right now we have to divert all of our attention and energy towards finding our final destination. We got no help from those creatures and I'm afraid that all we can rely on is the inscription on that metal plate."

"And that was inscribed some billion years after these colonies left Derevan," Curtar pointed out bluntly.

"I agree. It isn't going to be easy. As far as this race is concerned, we've been going further and further back in time with every step we've taken. Any changes in the exact position of Derevan have been magnified by an unknown amount as we've progressed closer to it."

"I think we should first all sleep on it after we've eaten," Viona said decisively. "Maybe after a few hours' rest, we'll all be thinking more clearly and logically. Now that we're outside that sun, away from that planet, there'll be nothing more to fear from those Derevanians."

As they ate, the Amazon gradually resumed her usual poise and good nature. Since they would be taking their directions for Derevan from this particular star, Abna set the automatic controls and they all retired to their couches. While they slept, the Ultra cruised in a stable orbit around the supergiant red sun, the electronic brains keeping it on its preprogrammed course.

* * * *

When they woke it was to find that Curtar was already awake and seated at the table in the observation well. He was turning something over and over in his hands, something which none of the others had ever seen before.

Staring down at it, the Amazon asked, "What is that, Curtar? Where did you find it?"

There was a strange expression on the Kezbekian's aged features as he replied, "Something has been troubling me ever since we took off from that first planet we visited. You remember that members of my race entered this spaceship and took away the obelisk. Then it occurred to me that, as well as doing that, they might have left something on board, so I carried out a search of this cabin—and found this."

He handed it carefully to the Amazon. It was a square metal box made of some heavy material, rather like a small camera. "I reckoned that since they had no idea when we would be returning, they wouldn't have much time in which to conceal it. It was clamped magnetically to the hull yonder." He pointed to the rear of the cabin.

"Do you know what it is?" Abna asked tightly.

Curtar nodded. "It's a tachyonic pulser. With this they can track you right across the galaxy, even when the Ultra is in hyperspace."

"What you're saying is that it emits pulses of tachyons?"

Nodding again, Curtar took the instrument back. "It's been sending out these pulses regularly ever since we left that world."

Mystified, Thania asked, "Just what are tachyons? I've never heard of them."

"Nor me," Mexone said.

Abna gave a wry smile. "As far as Earth scientists are concerned, tachyons are merely a hypothetical type of particle. No one there has yet proved that they even exist. Quite clearly, the scientists on Kezbek are further advanced than they are in this particular field of nuclear physics."

"Evidently you're talking about the Bilyanuk Hypothesis," the Amazon said. To the others, she went on, "Bilyanuk and his colleagues suggested that there are three different kinds of particles in the universe. They called these tardons, luxons and tachyons. The tardons are all of those particles that make up matter and antimatter. They have a positive rest mass—that is the mass they would have if they are completely at rest in the universe—and they can only travel below light velocity.

"The luxons are photons, neutrinos and their anti-particles. These have a zero rest mass and can only travel at the velocity of light."

"And these tachyons?" Viona asked, intensely interested.

"They have imaginary rest masses," the Amazon went on. "That is a mass multiplied by the square root of minus one. They only have positive masses when moving at velocities in excess of that of light.

Theoretically, a tachyon could cross the entire galaxy in virtually no time at all. Clearly, as far as the Kezbekian scientists are concerned, they've succeeded in isolating these elusive particles and have created this machine. With a suitable detector on board their planet or their spacecraft, they know exactly where the Ultra is."

"Then the sooner we destroy that instrument, the better," declared Mexone. "I suggest we fire it through one of he nuclear torpedo tubes. Once it's caught in that sun's gravitational field, we should see the last of it."

"That's exactly what I intend to do." The Amazon took the metal box and left the room. A few moments later they all saw it speeding away into the distance.

Coming back, she said decisively, "Now something to eat and then we plot a course for Derevan. There's nothing more we can learn from—"

The strident ringing of the ship's alarm broke in on her sentence. Whirling quickly, Abna muttered, "What now?"

"Somehow, I don't think this has anything to do with that race inside the sun," the Amazon called as she headed for the viewing screen. "This must be something else—something more urgent and dangerous."

Self-operated and connected to the radar, the alarm meant that something big had been picked up by the long-range system. Scanning the instruments, she said, "There's something almost directly ahead of us, a little over a million miles away. At the moment I can't determine what it is."

"There's no doubt it's coming towards us," Viona glanced over her mother's shoulder. "Somehow, it doesn't look like a solid image. See—it's made up of numerous tiny dots on the screen."

Abna threw it a quick glance. "You're absolutely right. That's an entire armada of spaceships. Anybody want to bet which planet they came from?"

"It would appear we were too late in destroying that pulser," Curtar said thinly. "They're from my own world, aren't they?"

The Amazon stared hard at him. "I'd say that's a foregone conclusion—and now we know how they have succeeded in following us across three quarters of the galaxy. They didn't really need the information written on that obelisk. They merely tracked us."

Her tone changed, became brisk and authoritative. "Right. Everybody to battle stations."

Swiftly, they took up their assigned positions. Very soon, the tiny dots of the enemy ships were apparent in the center of the screen. It was clear that this time the Kezbekians meant business.

Sucking in a deep breath, Viona said, "There must be forty or fifty vessels in that fleet. Surely we can't fight all of them?"

"We can have a damned good try," the Amazon snapped.

"Wouldn't it be better to try to reach top speed and slip into the fourth dimension?" Curtar suggested hopefully.

"That won't solve anything," The Amazon shook her head emphatically. "Even now they can no longer rely on that tachyon pulser to follow us, they still have the obelisk. I don't want to reach Derevan and find all of those vessels are still on our tail. I'm sure we can finish off most of them before we slip into hyperspace."

"All right, have it your way," Abna said. He knew that once this ruthless streak reached the surface nothing would sway her from her objective, regardless of the risk.

Checking that they all had their belts tightly about their waists, the Amazon turned to Curtar intending he should be safely strapped down on one of the couches but he shook his head.

"I'm still quite capable of handling one of these weapons," he said with a trace of indignation in his voice.

"All right, old man," said the Amazon, helping him into the seat at the controls of one of the protonic cannons. Within moments, he had a complete grasp of the controls, leaving the Amazon to return to her own place beside Abna.

The Kezbekian fleet headed straight for the Ultra without deviating from its tight, wedge-like formation. It was evident they knew that the Ultra carried far more powerful armaments than any of their vessels but, considering the odds, were confident of the outcome.

The Cosmic Crusaders waited tensely as the enemy approached. At the controls, the Amazon suddenly flicked a switch and the Ultra leapt forward. Easing back on another lever, she sent the spaceship into a tight climb until it was high above the oncoming vessels. The move took the enemy completely by surprise.

Three of the protonic cannons fired almost simultaneously. At the same time, Mexone sent two super-x-hydrogen shells spearing through the void. Both struck the leading vessel amidships. Twin vivid orange flashes showed at the points of impact. The searing atomic flame spread rapidly along the entire length of the spacecraft. Molten metal dripped into the void. A final gigantic explosion and the entire vessel disintegrated into radioactive dust.

Three other Kezbekian vessels were also falling out of space, spiraling towards the giant sun. Smiling grimly, the Amazon put the nose of the Ultra down and speared straight for the fleet. By now, the Crusaders, ably helped by Curtar, were firing at anything that came into their sights. Taken completely by surprise by the maneuver, the enemy vessels attempted to scatter.

Four more exploded in molten ruin and then the Ultra was through their midst, swinging round in a wide arc. The next moment, something utterly unexpected and incredible happened. For an instant, it seemed that the whole of space was lit up by an eye-searing white light. It utterly dimmed the orange-red light of the nearby sun.

Both the Amazon and Abna threw up their hands to cover their eyes, temporarily blinded by the vicious glare. The Ultra shuddered as the Amazon grappled with the controls, struggling to bring the ship back onto an even course. Slowly, the brilliance subsided and then faded altogether. The blackness of the void rushed back to take its place.

When they were able to see clearly again it was to find that the entire Kezbekian fleet had vanished. Not a single vessel was visible on the screen.

Thania stared incredulously through the port, unable to believe her eyes. "What in the cosmos was that?" the teenager asked in a strangled tone. She wiped the back of her hand over her streaming eyes. "It seemed to come from out of the sun. Surely it was too big and bright to be a prominence."

"It wasn't a prominence," the Amazon said quietly. "You all heard what those creatures on that planet said. Others have come here in the past and they have destroyed them. I think that's what just happened. Somehow they must have recognized them as enemies."

"Then all of them have been destroyed," Curtar said in a hushed whisper.

"Not all of them," Abna corrected. "Just before that happened, I noticed two of them vanish into hyperspace. Whatever weapon that was I doubt if it would touch them in the fourth dimension."

"You're certain they weren't caught in that blast?" Mexone asked.

"I'm positive. I've seen too many vessels at the instant when they warp into hyperspace not to recognize such a transition."

"Then almost certainly they're headed for Derevan," the Amazon put in. "Since we're now out of danger, that's what we have to do."

CHAPTER X

THE supergiant red sun and its equally strange world had faded into the distance by the time the Ultra approached the speed of light and was not indistinguishable from the myriad of others behind them. In the viewing screen the large majority of visible stars were already appearing bluer than normal as their light shifted towards the violet end of the spectrum due to the Doppler effect.

"Another five minutes and we'll be entering hyperspace," Abna said harshly. "I can't help wondering what we'll find at the end of the journey."

To Curtar, the Amazon said, "I suppose that for you this will be the ultimate fulfillment of the ambition of a lifetime. For us, it's been an adventure, not unlike most of the others we've had in the past. If we can learn anything from this race at least we'll have achieved something."

As they made their way amidships, Curtar said. "Whatever happens, I'd like to express my gratitude to you, Amazon, and all of the Cosmic Crusaders for giving me this chance. I doubt if I could have done it without you."

"You don't have to thank us, Curtar. To be quite honest, once you mentioned this primordial world where galactic life first began, it excited my scientific curiosity."

They lay down on their respective couches where the Amazon and Abna checked the controls and the final data that had been fed into the computer. Then everything was ready. Smoothly, the energy warp suffused the ship and they were, once again, in hyperspace.

* * * *

This time, when they emerged into normal space, the Ultra was deep inside one of the great spiral arms of the galaxy. Stars of every size and color blazed all around them. There were so many of them that Abna, standing in front of the controls with his hands clasped behind his back said, "This is not going to be easy, Vi. How do we differentiate the right sun from the thousands of others?"

"If we allow for the movement of stars over the last four billion years or so, at least the one we're looking for should be within four or five hundred light years, maybe even closer than that."

"Then it's going to be a case of trial and error. Let's take another look at that chart on the metal plate. After all, it's the only thing we have to help us."

Crossing to the table, they bent over the plate, studying it with the powerful magnifying glass. "There's nothing odd about the star itself," the Amazon said after a couple of minutes, "but there is what looks like a large cluster marked within a few light years of it."

Nodding soberly, Abna rubbed his chin. "That may not help us. It's a well-known fact that such clusters disperse appreciably after a few million years. That may not even exist now."

"I'm afraid I have to agree with you." The Amazon straightened up with a faint sigh of exasperation. "And since it's not marked as a double star, we can't use the computer in conjunction with the telescope as we did before."

Turning to face the others, she asked, "Do any of you have any suggestions?"

There was a long silence. Finally, Viona spoke: "I don't know if this will help but when we met those Derevanians on that last world they did make one remark which struck me as odd."

"Anything might help in this situation," Abna said. "Let's have it."

"They said that the radiation from that sun prevented them from achieving their final metamorphosis leaving them just as they are. Apart from that world in the Cygnus Rift where they were destroyed by a cosmic storm, I'd say this was also true of all those other suns we came across."

"Just what is it you're trying to say, Viona?" Mexone asked, still unable to see what his wife was getting at.

Viona spread her hands wide. "I'm suggesting that the original race left on Derevan did make that final change and that would mean that their sun is emitting some special kind of radiation which other suns aren't. If I'm right, it shouldn't be too difficult to scan these stars with the telescope and check on some kind of radiation not being emitted by any of the others."

The Amazon knit her brows in concentration before saying, "That shouldn't be too difficult. After all, we soon picked out that low-frequency radiation from that double star system."

Anxious to be doing something positive, Viona said quickly, "Then let's get started. Anything would be better than just standing here doing nothing but theorizing."

The Amazon quickly set the computer and as the telescope passed over each star, within nanoseconds, its entire spectrum of electromagnetic radiation was recorded. At the same time, the computer picked out any star that exhibited any anomalies in its spectrum. So rapidly did this system perform that the entire process took only five minutes.

They scanned the chart that was produced closely. Finally, Mexone said, "It seems we're in luck, Amazon. Only two stars have been picked out." He demonstrated with his finger.

"Just two," the Amazon mused, returning to the telescope with the chart in her hand. Deftly, she set the coordinates for the first. Seconds later, as she increased the magnification, it flashed onto the middle of the huge viewing screen above the controls.

Perusing it intently, Abna muttered finally, "I doubt if this can be the sun with Derevan in its system. It's emitting tremendous quantities of high-energy gamma rays which are lethal to any form of organic life."

"Any form of organic life as we know it," Viona pointed out. "But since we know so very little of the Derevanians, it's possible those rays have no effect on them."

Abna nodded in grudging assent. "You may be right, Viona. Let's examine that other candidate before we make up our minds. With those two Kezbekians vessels probably somewhere in this vicinity, we can't afford to waste time visiting them both."

The Amazon punched in the coordinates for the second star; then glanced at the computer data. "According to these figures, this one has a very peculiar emission spectrum."

Abna raised his brows. "Peculiar—in what way?"

"The visible part of the spectrum is present but as for the rest—"

Abna walked over, placed a hand on her shoulder, and glanced down at the figures. "I see what you mean, Vi. There are very few wavelengths being emitted beyond the ultraviolet. By far most of the radiation coming through is in the infrared and another intense band at very long wavelengths, far beyond the radio waves."

"Then that must be the star we're looking for," Thania said excitedly.

Finally, it was unanimously agreed that they should set course for this particular sun about a hundred and fifty light years away. As they strapped themselves in for the final trip through the fourth dimension, the Amazon heard Viona remark in a low voice, "We seem to be spending most of our time traveling through hyperspace on this trip."

"That's one of the problems of galactic travel, Viona. We've progressed a long way from the automobile and aircraft to crossing millions of light years of space."

* * * *

Less than ninety million miles away, a dull red color, the strange sun burned feebly against the eternal dark. It was slightly smaller than Sol—a very old star nearing the end of its life.

Seated in the observation well of the Ultra, they eyed their goal in silence. None of them doubted that this star represented the end of their search. Yet there was also an intense feeling of awe and satisfaction that they had located one star out of the teeming hundred billion suns that made up the great spiral of the Milky Way galaxy.

The Amazon suddenly pushed herself to her feet. "Well, now we're here we'd better start looking for this planet. At the moment, I don't see any."

While Abna reduced their tremendous forward velocity, the others crowded to the viewing screen and observation ports, searching the region around the dull sun for any sign of tiny crescents that would indicate the whereabouts of any attendant worlds.

"I can see three of them!" Thania yelled, jumping up and down with excitement. "Two large ones and a smaller one closer to the sun."

After studying them closely with the telescope, the Amazon said: "You're right, Thania. The two outer ones are clearly gas giants like

Jupiter. The other appears more like Earth. As far as I can make out it has an atmosphere."

"Derevan," Curtar muttered. There was an expression of wonder on his lined face. "I never thought it possible."

Turning, the Amazon smiled. "You've experienced a lot in your long lifetime, Curtar. I only hope, for your sake, that this is the right world."

"It is," the Kezbekian nodded excitedly. "I can feel it."

Ignoring the two outer planets, they guided the Ultra sunward, approaching the small planet from the night side. As they neared it, they immediately noticed something strange about this world.

"The shape is all wrong," Thania cried, peering through the telescope. "It seems to be oddly twisted and lop-sided. What can that mean?"

After a quick look for himself, Abna said, "So that's the answer."

"The answer to what?" the Amazon queried.

"To all the other worlds we found; all had been traveling through space without an attendant sun. It seemed too big a coincidence to be merely chance. Now we have the answer here, right in front of our eyes. Some billions of years ago, Derevan was a much larger planet but something catastrophic happened and it split into pieces. Four segments were sent flying off into space, carrying any survivors with them."

"That certainly makes sense," Mexone agreed. "And countless years later they were all captured by other stars—all except the first one we found in the Cygnus Dark Rift."

"There's something else I've noticed about this planet," stated the Amazon. "If you look closely you'll see that even the night side, where it should be totally dark, has a faint albedo."

"It could be due to radioactivity," Viona suggested. "I'll check with the radiation detector."

Operating on a principle similar to long-range radar, the beam struck the distant surface and was then reflected back to the Ultra—but strangely the instrument remained silent. There were only a few desultory clicks, but these were due to stray cosmic radiation from space.

"Definitely not radioactive," she said, concealing her disappointment at being proved wrong.

"Then there's only one other answer," the Amazon said. "The whole of that hemisphere must be covered either with ice or carbon dioxide snow."

"Indicative of a very low temperature," Abna added. "We'd better check the conditions down there before we land. I wouldn't like to put the Ultra down into a hundred feet of ice or snow."

The results were soon obtained. The atmosphere was not unlike that of Earth, with 81 percent of oxygen and the rest almost all nitrogen.

"There's also about two percent helium present but that shouldn't prove a problem."

Mexone said: "The temperature at the surface is four degrees below zero. Not a very nice world at night—and judging from the radiation from that sun I doubt if it's much warmer during the daytime."

Moving in a circular orbit about the planet, Abna finally put the Ultra down not far from the terminator on the sunlit side. Details were clearly visible through an atmosphere that seemed to be completely devoid of clouds.

Descending the ladder in their thermally heated suits, they stepped down onto a strange world. Around the large clear space were numerous buildings with classic lines.

Tall, carved pillars supported wide roofs. Long streets ran in all directions with stone fountains in the numerous squares and plazas.

But it was a bitter, arctic world—a seemingly dead world. Everything was covered in thick sheets of translucent ice. Long icicles draped the walls and openings. The silence of long ages hung over the scene.

Staring around her through the transparent mask of her suit, the Amazon said harshly,

"This is certainly not what I expected to find. There's been no life here for countless millennia."

Lifting her head, she looked towards the curiously distorted horizon. Slowly, she turned to face Curtar who now seemed utterly bewildered and lost. "I'm sorry. If the Deveranians were truly immortal, they must have left here countless ages ago. Either because their world became too cold—or for some other reason we'll probably never know."

"I understand." There was an ineffable sadness in his low voice. "It would seem I was expecting too much—far too much."

Thania suddenly spoke up, breaking in on their conversation. "So it's seems to be a dead world but that shouldn't stop us taking a look around. We might find some answers in those buildings yonder." She was already walking away as she spoke, picking her way carefully over the hard-packed ice.

The others followed in silence.

There was very little ice inside the nearest building and they could see clearly in the pale red sunlight streaming through the many apertures in the walls. There was a long table down the center but no chairs. Along each side was a low rail.

"Being more of an avian than a human species it appears they had no need of chairs," the Amazon commented. "Evidently they preferred to perch on this rail as they ate."

"Some of them were certainly excellent artists," Abna observed, pointing to the high walls. "Those pictures appear to depict scenes from their early evolution and this one—" he pointed to the last mural, "—is obviously intended to represent the disruption of their planet."

The image was stark and awesome, showing a world torn to pieces by some form of internal disruption.

The Amazon pursed her lips, before remarking: "It doesn't make a pretty picture, does it?"

For almost half an hour, they wandered through the deserted buildings and empty, silent streets before returning to where they had left the Ultra. By now, night had fallen in earnest. Only the faint shimmer of starlight glittered on the ice. Slowly, they made their way to where the ladder hung from the airlock—then stopped at a sudden cry from Viona who was a short distance behind them.

"What under the stars is that?"

Swiftly, they all turned. A brilliant white glow showed on the horizon. It brightened perceptively as they watched in awe and wonderment, dimming the light of the stars.

"It can't be a moon—we never saw one!" Thania exclaimed.

"Perhaps it's something like your aurora borealis, Vi," Abna suggested. "An electrical phenomenon due to charged particles from the sun interacting with atoms in the upper atmosphere."

Slowly, it rose into the black heavens—a huge shining column of light that came moving towards them over the uneven ground.

"That is certainly not the aurora borealis," the Amazon gasped. "There's a definite purpose behind its movement."

Almost a mile high, the glowing column stopped when it was about two hundred yards away. Tiny silver motes like a horde of fireflies danced and gyrated within it.

We are the Derevanians. The awesome voice echoed within their minds.

You have met with others of our race during your journey here but we alone have achieved the final metamorphosis that was our destiny. We possess all the knowledge of the galaxy. It was we who, in the beginning, seeded all of the suitable worlds with life so that intelligence might evolve throughout the entire length and breadth of the galaxy.

Some, who progressed more quickly than you, have come here seeking knowledge only for their own evil ends. They have never returned to their own worlds. You are the first to come who seek knowledge only for its own sake. Others have destroyed their own worlds and themselves through greed and the lust for power.

"We seek neither of these things," the Amazon cried. For the first time in her life, she realized she was up against something far beyond her imagining. Their weapons, powerful as they were, were of no use against this apparition.

That we already know, came the thunderous intonations in their minds.

Speaking loudly, Abna called, "But there are others following us and they—"

We know of them too. They are no longer a threat—either to us or to you. They have been destroyed. Five of you are already gifted with virtual immortal lives. Your journeying through the galaxy has been noted and we find no evil in it.

The sixth among you is old according to his race and we have foreseen that he will never live to return to his own world. He will therefore be given both knowledge and immortality.

None of the Cosmic Crusaders were fully aware of what happened next. They had a brief glimpse of Curtar standing a few feet away. The next moment there was a sudden glare of incandescent flame that engulfed him completely. For a few moments it completely blinded them.

Blinking rapidly, the Amazon saw that the Kezbekian was no longer there. In his place was a small glowing pillar of light, one that began to drift slowly upward and away from them. Instants later it melted into the gigantic pillar.

There—it is done, boomed the stupendous voice. *As for the five of you, we leave you to return to your journeying among the stars. You will find there is now sufficient fuel for your vessel. Before you go, we wish to thank you. We have read your minds, and in particular the mind of one amongst you known as Viona. We were astounded to learn of her journey to the very center of the universe, and how she communed with the Central Intelligence itself, who used her as an instrument to utterly destroy her evil former husband, Sefner Quorne!*

Eons ago, a group of our scientists made a similar journey, hoping to discover the secrets of the universe, and the underlying reason or cause for the infinity of universes that exist. They never returned, and the experiment was abandoned.

It appeared to us that our universe and others had been conceived without purpose, and would continue in the same way until its unfathomable and causeless end. We therefore concluded that creation was purely random. But now we know why our ancestors never returned! They must have been utterly destroyed by the Central Intelligence, as was Quorne!

Our earlier conclusion that there is no reason behind the universe or anything in it, now needs to be modified. From Viona's subconscious mind we were able to read an actual message from the Central Intelligence itself. She herself did not remember it directly, but I will repeat it for you now: 'For every universe there is a unit such as I, and there are universes without number within each other and without each other, all of them embedded in a Supreme One whom none can understand or fathom'.

There may—or may not—be a purpose to the creation of our universe, but that purpose must remain forever unknowable, so that to all intents and purposes, our universe and everything in it appears to exist purely by chance. These revelations from Viona are of profound interest to us, and we will brood on them for cycles to come. And that is all we can tell you.

There was no indication that the glittering column had turned but slowly, completely soundlessly, it began to drift away, finally vanishing below the horizon. Overhead, the stars appeared with their usual brilliance.

After a moment's awkward silence, Abna said in a hushed tone: "You know, I think we've just be in the presence of something close to the gods. The supreme indigenous intelligence in the galaxy. It makes me realize just how insignificant we really are when compared to beings like that."

"I suppose it does," the Amazon said. "Compared with them the Mizanu we encountered in the Alpha Centauri system was nothing—and it was the epitome of evil. At least, the Derevanians could show benevolence when they wished."

One by one they climbed the ladder and entered the Ultra, closing the airlock behind them. When they were all seated with Abna and the Amazon at the controls, Thania looked at Viona. There was something like awe in her voice as she spoke:

"I always knew that you must have had some remarkable adventures, Viona, but I never suspected anything like that! To have traveled to the very center of the universe…" She shot a guilty glance at Mexone, and lowered her voice, "Nor that you had another husband before Mexone…"

Viona smiled faintly. "Quorne was never really my husband, Thania. It's a long story, and one I prefer to forget, but maybe one day I'll tell you about it."

Thania said in a low voice: "Thank you. I didn't mean to pry…" Then in a louder tone she added: "I don't know about the rest of you, but what the Derevanians told us has left me feeling depressed—that we can never discover the reason behind the universe or anything in it. That everything seems to happen purely by chance."

For a moment, the Amazon remained silent. Then she said briskly, "Then there's only one way to cure depression—to continue with our work, go out there among the stars and carry on helping those less fortunate than ourselves."

"And where do you suggest we should go now?" Abna asked, a faint smile on his lips.

The Amazon gave a short laugh. "Just point the nose of the Ultra in any direction you like. I'm sure that we'll discover something both intriguing and exciting—if we just leave it to chance."